"What the hell was he waiting for?"

Vaiking wondered to himself. He had shot captives before. She was only an Indian, a squaw. Why not? Still he hesitated.

"I'm gettin' to be a hell of a soldier," he muttered.

The woman stirred, glanced up at him, then resumed her stoical waiting. Vaiking drew his pistol and slowly cocked it. The woman neither moved nor flinched. The big, blond soldier aimed the muzzle at her rounded, black-haired skull. His finger tightened against the trigger. Then it relaxed.

Slowly he uncocked the pistol and holstered it.

BROKEN LANCE

X.X. Jones

BALLANTINE BOOKS · NEW YORK

I

The column was businesslike, but absurdly brief. It shuffled among the choppy hills toward the Cimarron, a floating blue island of thirty-four men and their leg-weary horses, ten pack mules and two packers, the total about half the size designated by the Table of Organizations, a fiction perpetrated annually by the War Department. But, under-strength or not, it was proud and all military, for it was K Company, 12th Cavalry. Two-thirds of its troopers had been blooded in the war a couple of years past and gone, save in their everlasting, flowering memories.

"A hell of a command," grumbled Captain Karl Ravalier, brevet Lieutenant Colonel, riding at the head of it, and reflecting on its size, more than anything. First Sergeant Joel Vaiking, to his left and the correct two paces to the rear, squinted warily at the heat-quivering skyline all about, flicked his gray gaze down the bobbing outfit, and agreed. "A hell of a command, sir." But he thought of other things, and his inflection differed. The officer flashed a grin, baring a snaggle of yellowed teeth below the sweep of a brown horseman's mustache.

"Okay, Sergeant," he said. "Anyway, it's what we're down to now."

He blasted a sigh, longing for the days of mighty

operations and commands more suitable for one of his dash and competence, both wasted on abbreviated units and police details out on these goddam endless plains. A man would have to stir up a general outbreak to properly exercise talents honed sharp in a great war. You could never maintain a reputation, and build on it, filling out reports and chasing shadows. Twenty-eight days on this scout, clear to hell and gone past the Republican to the Platte and back, and not a fight nor a sign of an Indian fresh enough to warm up Dipsy Jack.

But that suited Sergeant Vaiking just fine. He had had a bellyful of fighting, beginning after his abbreviated career at West Point with Shiloh and through Gettysburg, where his Medal of Honor hardly compensated for five weeks in a stinking hospital, and then to the Wilderness and Five Corners. It was okay with him if he never fought again forever. He squared his massive shoulders and reset the kepi on his blond hair which was matted wet where the band of his hat had pressed and long from a month without the attention of the company barber. He had been a soldier more than a quarter of his twenty-seven years and couldn't imagine anything but Army life. Rough, all right, but a good life, some of the time. No future, but a man didn't have to worry about that, either. He did his job, obeyed orders and settled for today, each day.

That was what he thought, about himself and his job, when he considered it at all, but the men of K Company saw him differently. Vaiking was K Company to them, the reason why some of them stayed in the Army at all. He was why K Company was professional, a good fighting outfit, one you could be proud of.

Vaiking would have guessed that few men reflected much on a soldier's life. Most were like Nero that way. Buck Sergeant Ravel Nero. Bony Nero. A fair noncom, but an odd man, one who actually enjoyed the killing and all that. A peculiar man.

Vaiking glanced back down the column. Beyond he packs Nero had reined in alongside a horse whose rider, dismounted, was inspecting a front hoof. The trooper straightened, looked at Nero who gestured, and started out after the command, walking, leading a horse Vaiking's practiced eye could see, even from this distance, was limping. Nero again brought up the rear.

"Riley's horse's gone lame, sir," reported Vaiking. "He's leadin'."

"Oh, hell," sighed Ravalier. He signaled for a halt. Time for a break, anyway. The men fell out. A few lighted stubby pipes. There was little talking; there never was much to say on the tail end of a long scout. Vaiking rode back to where Danny Riley plodded up, leading his limping roan.

"Where th' hell you find a rock on these mud prairies, Danny?" he grunted. Riley grinned his easy smile. He liked the First Sergeant.

"Old Snuffle could find one in th' middle of th' ocean," he said cheerfully. "I'd like to drop him in it, too, was we there."

"Better let Mannstein look at it," advised Vaiking. "Maybe he can fix him up so's you can ride. It beats walking." Mannstein had once studied to be a veterinarian. He was good with stock.

Vaiking joined Ravalier, sitting glumly in the shade of his horse. If he was thinking of anything the officer didn't mention it. The brass-eagle buttons on his blue coat were undone three or four down from the throat, to let in what air was moving. The sweat stains under his arms were rimmed with white from the salts of his body. Ravalier wore no shirt under his blouse, nor did any of the men. Too hot. His clothes were wrinkled, dusty and worn, but they seemed trim on him, nonetheless. He was an officer.

A speck, dragging a plume of dust, burst from the breaks, a mile or two ahead of the column.

"Captain, sir, yonder comes Dipsy Jack," announced Vaiking, a lift in his voice. "Seems in a rush. Maybe found something."

Ravalier bounced to his feet, peered across his horse at

the rider pounding toward them, then swept into the saddle, all business.

"Mount 'em up, Sergeant!" he ordered briskly. "Let's go! It looks like action. At last."

He jogged ahead to meet the scout. Gone was boredom, lethargy. He was a soldier, now, the kind men would eagerly follow.

"Injuns, Gin'l!" called Dipsy Jack, his lush raven beard split to reveal a wide grin and mouthful of white teeth. He called all officers General, he once explained, because with so many brevets he didn't rightly know one true rank from another, "an' none of 'em gets mad at being' called Gin'l."

"A whole damn camp, comin' in to water jes' over that furtherest ridge! Cheyennes! An' they ain't many dog soldiers aroun'. Must be out huntin'. Oh, suwannee, kin we make a sweep of 'um!"

He was tickled as a kid with a new paint pony.

Behind them the troopers came on at a fast trot. Riley had mounted his horse, which still limped, but was keeping pace. Nero had the rear of the column up tight. You could depend on him, time like this.

Dipsy Jack led the way down through a clay gorge to the sand bed of the Cimarron, a sprinkling of cottonwoods lining the course of what usually was a stream, in weather wet enough to feed it. Nothing now but pools of buffalo-yellowed water. Ravalier halted the command just short of one of them, and sent the scout and Vaiking to reconnoiter. From the protection of a cutbank they peered through stubby, strong-smelling sage at a straggling mass of travois, women, ponies and dogs, with a few men as outriders, tumbling through the hills a couple of miles distant, coming this way, making for the river.

"Must be thirty-five, mebbe fifty lodges," estimated Dipsy Jack. He squinted at the horde, calculatingly. "Looks like Dust Devil's band, but I don't see him nor High Back Rib. Thar's Big Ass, though, on thet calico to th' right!"

Vaiking glimpsed a heavy Indian halted on the low knoll.

"See us?" he wondered.

"Tain't likely," Jack turned to aim a watery brown stream from his last chew at an unsuspecting rock. "Jes' cautious, is all. You cain't hardly surprise 'em ever—th' way we goin' ter do."

Vaiking skidded down the bank, caught up his horse and reported to the Captain. The officer showed the decisiveness and élan which had brought him such fame during the war. His one brown eye now had the tic over it, the sole sign of nervous tension on the officer's lean face, but both it and its brilliant blue mate were alive, seeing the situation, the terrain, the possibilities, the needs. He split the company, holding one wing behind an outcropping on the near side of the buffalo trace down which the camp would have to come, and sending the other, with Jack and under Vaiking, to a like position beyond it. When the Indians filed into the bottomlands they would be caught in a murderous vise.

"Never mind your tracks, Sergeant," he hissed. "Time they see 'em it'll be too goddam late. Come out mounted when I do!" Vaiking nodded and led off. A mounted attack was a rarity in Indian fighting, but it would be a good thing here. With any kind of luck the soldiers could cut the Indian camp in two and roll up either part. The confusion would help. The Indians can't stand confusion, Jack often pointed out. Mix them up and you have them half whipped.

Dipsy Jack all but quivered with anticipation. He ducked back as Big Ass, riding lighter on his spotted pony than one would expect, appeared on the bluff above the stream, scanning it before the people filed down, seeing whether it appeared barren of enemies. The soldiers, concealed beyond his vision, waited tensely. The Indian disappeared, and shortly down through the narrow buffalo gap scrambled the caravan, a jumbled mass of milling horses, shouting women, a clanging kettle or two, twisted travois and tepee poles, and dust-raising herds of stock. The bottomlands, apparently empty of life but a moment ago, now were tumultuous with a seething, chattering busy throng of people and animals, making first for the waterholes.

Like a thunderclap—not in volume, but in discordance—

came a trumpet peal from beyond the mob and the thin line of blue riders swept out toward the Indian mass. Vaiking led his own men on a slashing attack from the other side, blasting through the screaming camp whose attention had been drawn the other way by the peal of the brass horn.

Outnumbered, it was the dash, the surprise, the thundering impact of the twin charges that burst through the confused complex of shouting, terrified Indians, raising a dust so that you could scarcely tell a red foe from a white ally; but the troopers, carried by their momentum into the throng, blasted with their pistols, hacked with sabers, spearing, jabbing, thrusting. This was work. This was what they were in business for. They were silent, sweating automatons, swift in motion, remorseless in execution, relentless, laying steel on flesh, cutting, stabbing, shooting, with only the squeals of the fleeing women, the whoops of an occasional warrior who still fought back, the wail of a child, the blast of a wounded horse sounding above the fury of the assault. Vaiking's troopers burst through, whirled, joined the Captain's men and fought back into the mob. Vaiking sabered down an Indian with a tomahawk raised over the back of Ravalier's head, earning a quick grin of thanks from the officer. And then the fight was over, troopers galloping this way and that, chasing fluttering squaws and fleeing men, cutting down the last they could come up with, the bottomlands a hopeless litter of abandoned goods of the destroyed community.

"Recall, Henry!" bellowed Ravalier. "Blow the recall!"

The clear notes of the trumpet, sounding fresh and unmoved by all the slaughter, rose above the bottomlands, and slowly the troopers guided their lathered horses back to where the Captain and Vaiking sat, surveying the carnage. Ravalier was in a fine mood, the battle-elation still upon him.

Riley was one of the last to arrive, his roan still limping, but not so much in all the combat-fever. The Irishman prodded before him a woman, wrapped in a trade blanket, her raven braids dusty, her face streaked and sullen, her black eyes expressionless. Young, thought Vaiking. None of the fat of middle-aged squaws. Might be pretty, cleaned up. Riley motioned her over to where the Captain and Sergeant sat their quivering horses in the shade of a cottonwood. The pack train came up the bottom from where it had been held, out of sight, and joined the gathering command.

"Found this'un in the brush, Captain, sir," explained Riley. "Thought you might like to talk with 'er."

The officer looked the woman over speculatively. Dipsy Jack spoke a few sentences to her, in the guttural, throaty tongue of the Cheyennes.

"Belongs to Dust Devil," he said. "His woman. Says she don't know where he is at. Says she don't know nothin', an' I reckon they ain't no way of rootin' out anythin' she mought know."

Ravalier surveyed the scene once more. He glanced at the evening sky, bit his mustache, as he looked up- and downstream. His exhilaration still burned brightly, flushing his face, enlivening his odd eyes, but the tic was gone from over the brown one.

"Likely the fighting men will hit us tonight?" he asked Jack. The scout shook his head.

"They won't be gathered tonight, or know what's happened. They mought give us hell tomorrow, while we is headin' fer the post, or next day. But not tonight, Gin'l, though it'd be best to have a double guard, seems to me."

Ravalier nodded.

"Vaiking," he said then, "have my tent set up under that cottonwood. Get supper. Maybe if the men root around among all that wreckage they can find some buffalo meat, which'd be a change. Let that woman clean up. After supper bring her to my tent. I want to—ah—talk with her."

"You want Jack to interpret, sir?" asked Vaiking, knowing the answer before it came.

"No," said Ravalier.

II

"I don't reckon," murmured Riley solicitously to his bunkie, Ole Swanson, as they turned in, "that the Captain will get much sleep tonight."

"Poor son of a bitch," agreed Swanson. "That's the only advantage I see to bein' a officer, havin' a tent an' all."

"Yeah," replied Riley. "I'd sure admire to git some of that 'all.'"

Matt Gunderson shared duty with George Morris on the doubled guard upstream. Their post, in the deep shade of a clump of trees, was out of sight of the picket line, but within hearing.

"We got to make real sure," he said sarcastically, after the detail had been established, "that the ol' man ain't disturbed. Needs his rest."

Morris snickered.

"Might be rest he needs, but I bet it ain't rest he's gittin'," he said.

Ravalier shouldered out of his tent in the faint dawn, adjusting his trousers and looking as rested as though he had slept the night through. Sheets of heavy wood smoke lay in the valley like water lapping against the clay banks. The

Captain summoned Vaiking and Dipsy Jack and questioned them over coffee. Jack opined the Cheyennes might strike the command on the way to the post, two days or more distant, "but agin, they mought not. You cain't hardly tell about what they is goin' ter do, except expect them to do somethin' unlikely, an' to do her fast an' hard."

The strikers moved in on the tent, dropping it in billowing folds of canvas. Vaiking, wondering at himself, found a cup and took coffee to the squaw, sitting cross-legged under her blanket, saying nothing, unmoving, her gaze from unblinking eyes fixed on the ground before her. He left the steaming coffee beside her, formed up the men and got them into the saddle, awaiting orders from the Captain who was busily writing in his journal and unfolding the map on which he had made an occasional note during the long scout.

At last he put the notebook away, folded the map and returned it to his saddle pocket, mounted his horse and indicated to K Company that it was to move out. He summoned Vaiking with a jerk of his head, nodded to the woman, still sitting cross-legged on the ground, her red blanket wrapped tightly around her slender body. The coffee, the Sergeant noted, was untouched.

"Shoot her," ordered Ravalier, and spurred away to lead the column out. It wound off, down the river bottom, through the cottonwoods.

Vaiking watched it disappear. He folded his hands on the pommel of his McClellan, glanced at the squaw, who seemed unaware of him, and remained immobile, silent. What the hell was he waiting for? the Sergeant wondered. Shooting a prisoner, what of that? He was a soldier. He had shot captives before, under orders or because some situation demanded it, and never thought anything about it or, if he had, it was a long, long time ago and he couldn't clearly recall the occasion. Killing a woman? She was only an Indian. Many a plainsman claimed the women were more bloodthirsty than the men, so it wasn't as if he had been ordered to shoot a white woman. He wouldn't do that, of course. But a squaw, now, why not?

Still he hesitated.

"I'm gettin' to be a hell of a soldier," he muttered to himself.

The woman stirred, glanced up at him, then resumed her stoical waiting. For what, she did not know. She probably knew what he had to do, Vaiking thought. Of course. She must be aware of it.

Vaiking drew his pistol and slowly cocked it. The woman neither moved nor flinched. She only waited. The big, blond soldier lowered the muzzle until it was aligned with her rounded, black-haired skull. His finger tightened against the trigger. Then it relaxed.

He uncocked the pistol and holstered it. He ran his hand across his eyes, stroked the raspy stubble on his unshaven chin, and stared again down the riverbed to the bend where the column had disappeared. He looked once more at the squaw, and slowly shook his head, as much in disbelief at himself as anything. He couldn't understand his action, or inaction, rather.

"Woman!" he called. She looked up at him, through him, from somewhere beyond the depths of her black eyes. Vaiking nodded upstream, past the tangled jumble of yesterday's action, indicating she was to go. Her eyes widened slightly, perhaps with surprise, then narrowed as she pondered whether this might be another white man's trick. Vaiking gestured again, impatiently. She lithely gained her feet, threw him a glance which might have been anything save gratitude, clutched the blanket still more tightly to her body. Head bowed, she waded away through the sand drifts.

Vaiking watched her go. Her jerked his horse around, and cantered downstream after the command.

He caught up a mile below, where it had stopped for the usual first break to adjust equipment and settle into the routine. Vaiking walked his horse to the outfit's head, where the Captain was conversing with Dipsy Jack under a sprawling tree. Their horses browsed among the fallen leaves, but the Sergeant mechanically noted that Ravalier, the master of military efficiency, had not neglected to post his guards. This was enemy country.

"Jack thinks if we cut back up on top we can make for the post direct," explained the officer. "That way we can save a few miles and the Cheyennes would be hard put to surprise us."

The Sergeant nodded.

"Well," said Ravalier, struggling to his feet, "let's try it."

He looked quizzically up at Vaiking, still sitting his horse.

"Any difficulty with your mission, Sergeant?"

Vaiking hesitated. He wondered whether this was a time to tell the truth or take a soldier's out. But essentially he was an honest man.

"I didn't shoot her, Captain," he said.

Ravalier's mouth tightened. His gaze narrowed until the brown all but disappeared and only the brilliant blue eye shone, a level, chilling stare.

"Say again, Sergeant. I don't hear good in the mornings."

"I let her go, sir."

"Why, for God's sake?"

"I don't know, Captain."

"You been in the Army long enough to recognize an order, Sergeant? You know what it means to disobey one? *Nero!*" He fairly bellowed the name. Nero loped up, tugging his horse to a standstill and, aware of the officer's mood, saluting sharply.

"Yes, sir?"

"Nero," said the Captain, in his cold fury, "take Jack with you back to the bivouac. Track down that squaw, Dust Devil's woman. Shoot her. I don't care if she found her way to half the Cheyenne nation already. Kill her! That's an order, Sergeant!"

Nero grinned through his black, stubbly whiskers.

"Yes, *sir*," he said. He and Jack galloped out on the back trail, upstream, disappearing among the trees.

"Disobeying an order is a serious thing, Vaiking, in time of war," repeated the Captain thoughtfully, unable, or unwilling, to let the matter drop. He was slightly confused himself, although he dared not show it, uncertain about his own motives, questioning for the first time his action. "This *is* war," he said once again, as if arguing with himself. "Even if Congress don't say it is."

"I know, sir," admitted Vaiking, resignedly.

Ravalier turned the incident over once more in his mind. Then he turned his hostile stare at his First Sergeant again.

"Get into the ranks, Private Vaiking," he decided, "and let me think this through again."

Without a word, Vaiking wheeled his horse and rode down the column, every man of which had heard the interchange, or part of it anyway, and knew he had been busted; feeling for him, but embarrassed to show it, and not wanting to embarrass Vaiking, either. But he could feel their unity with him and it warmed him, even if it added to the confusion in his own mind.

The command turned left and followed an old trace made by the hoofs of thousands of buffalo in years past, up through the mud banks, gaining the empty prairies after half an hour or so. Nero and Jack had not yet caught up. Ravalier checked his compass, squinted at the sun, and led off to the northeast. The plains seemed lifeless. Not even an antelope showed itself. The troopers rode silent as ghosts, no singing, not much talking, no joking or even cursing. Ahead of them, short of the trooper at the point by a quarter of a mile, rode Ravalier, his muscular back silently rolling with the steady gait, but the Captain not looking around, knowing the command was there, but saying nothing, mute, an unbridgeable gap between him, as a commissioned officer, and the enlisted soldiers. The man was apart because of rank. He was apart for other reasons, as well.

After an hour the column halted for its second break, the troopers sprawling on either side of the route, the lucky ones, having still a bit of tobacco, lighting up their worn and blackened pipes, the others envious. Vaiking rode to a slight knoll, with the plains open all around, finding there a patch of uncropped buffalo grass and sat in the middle of it, letting his horse graze the rich growth around him, nickering its pleasure, ripping the grass off with comfortable, tearing sounds. Joel still was troubled by his earlier action, but thought very little about being reduced in grade. He did not blame the officer. He blamed himself. He could not be sure where lay his fault, however. For not killing the squaw? For telling the Captain he hadn't shot her? Maybe a little of both. Riley drifted over and sat beside him, lending him the only thing he had, his sympathy.

"It ain't right, Sarge," he said. "I ain't been in the Army too long, but I think you done right an' got done wrong by."

"It's all soldierin'," replied Vaiking, without bitterness. There was a philosophical touch in his comment, perhaps.

He glanced down their back trail and saw two distant dots coming along, Nero and Jack. He started to tell Ravalier, then decided not to. He wasn't the noncom any more. It was none of his business.

The Captain shortly observed the oncoming pair himself, and held the command past the end of the break, waiting for them to catch up. Nero led the way to the officer, and sat his sweating horse while he checked in.

"Find her?" demanded Ravalier.

"Found her, sir," replied Nero. "She hadn't reached her people yet." He paused a moment, then answered the Captain's unasked question: "We shot 'er."

"You're acting First Sergeant, Nero," said Ravalier, with vast relief. "Mount 'em up. We wasted time enough already this morning. We better move or we'll get caught out here where there's no place for a stand."

Dipsy Jack, getting no other orders, fell in beside the officer. Ravalier favored this bulky plainsman, getting a

boot out of hearing him gabble on about his intricate past—
Indians, game, anything about which he might, for the
moment, be concerned. In addition to that, he was as fine a
scout as any on the government rolls, brave, reliable, and
with a native cunning Ravalier found highly useful. The two
shared parallel views toward fighting and redskins, and
living beyond the frontier. Both believed in taking what
they could, and making the best of what they could not
grasp. Jack felt freer with the officer than an enlisted man
could. They rode in companionable silence for a quarter
hour or more.

"Purty li'l thing, she was," Dipsy said reflectively,
thinking of the squaw.

"Just an Indian, Jack," said Ravalier shortly.

"She was, at that," agreed the scout. "I married one,
oncet. Not a Cheyenne, a 'Rapahoe—they is better cooks.
She was purty, too, I thought."

"What became of her?" the Captain wondered idly.

"I wonder, too," admitted Jack. "I just married her fer a
season, you mought say. Come snow I went south an' never
seemed to git aroun' to goin' back. I think I got 'er with
foal, but never heerd fer sure."

The Captain laughed.

"How many squaws you got 'with foal,' Jack?" he
challenged. His chameleon-like mood had flipped to high
good humor, now that his last night's adventure had been,
he thought, permanently erased.

"Hell, Gin'l, I don't rightly know, but they's been several
I suspect," said Dipsy Jack.

Ravalier turned in the saddle and peered thoughtfully
along their back trail, and at the horizon all around. The
command seemed the only animation on the plains, that
early morning.

"I don' think they is too much to worry about, Gin'l,"
said Jack. "We found 'er in the brush, but dragged 'er into
th' open arter we shot 'er, an' when Dust Devil finds 'er,
he'll have to take care of mournin' 'er afore he kin come
arter us, an' thet won't be until we gits back."

The pair rode silently for a few minutes, the comradeship still between them. Ravalier and Jack did not pretend they were equals, and understood their proper relationship, but on occasions such as this they could communicate on something of an even plane.

"Ain't no reason to worry about what th' Army'll say, Gin'l?" Jack diplomatically asked.

"None," replied the officer, flatly. "The Army don't care anything about such matters, so long as the Indian lovers don't hear of it and become aroused. They'll never learn about it this time any more than they have in the past. Vaiking is a soldier, and won't talk. Nero is First Sergeant now and he can't talk or he'll lose his grade, and he knows it. I'm not going to say anything, and I know you won't."

Jack grinned his whisker-splitting grin.

"Right as you kin be, Gin'l," he said. "If I tol' all I know I'd have time fer nothin' but talk talk talk. Anyways, I veer to one side or t'other of th' truth so common, no one knows fer sure when I'm speakin' fact or factless. Mebbe it's none of my business, but you fixin' to court-martial Vaiking?"

"You're right as hell," snapped Ravalier. "It's none of your goddam business!" The pair rode on in silence, Jack waiting for the officer to switch subjects, and Ravalier's mind in a turmoil set off by the scout's question. "Maybe he will be, and maybe not," he mused, after a time.

Jack took it as an opening for him to enter once again.

"You kin bust him without sayin' why," he pointed out, "but if you court-martial him you got to say why, an' mebbe the Army couldn't dodge the question then."

Ravalier looked sharply at him, a slow smile gradually spreading over his hawkish face.

"You sly bastard," he admired grudgingly.

III

The scattering of buildings, most of them fashioned of adobe, a few of timber and one of brick, looked unmilitary enough, but the Army persisted in calling it Fort Arnold Chopps, after a noted Civil War General, killed along the Chattahoochee, although the layout had been created before the war. Naturally, the enlisted men, when they felt kindly toward it, which was not too frequently, referred to the place as Fort Chips, or Fort Buffalo Chips, and when they were less gracious, under a coarser name.

Fort Chips had been laid out by orthodox Army planners when their vision outran their means. It had been conceived as a six-company post, properly outfitted, before the Civil War when it was thought that guarding the overland trails was likely to be the main task of the Army as far ahead as a man could see. Nobody, obviously, would ever *settle* the plains. People would just have to cross them to get to where they wanted to settle, or mine, or establish themselves. That was why Chips was built near the Santa Fe Trail.

However, after the war there had not been the manpower or, for that matter, the hard cash, to maintain Chips as originally planned, and it usually was garrisoned by at most three companies, and sometimes, by one alone. It had become, in short, more of a picket post than a regular fort,

16

and likely would continue as such until more funds were available. Normally, however, it had two companies stationed there, but the day before K returned, E of the 12th Cavalry had left on a scout to the south with orders to report in at Fort Larned, to the east, on conclusion of its mission. Some other company probably would be assigned to join K at Chips, but, Army communications being what they were, no one knew when that might be. All Ravalier had been informed officially was that he and K were to garrison Chips alone temporarily, and "temporarily" might mean a lifetime, or what would seem a lifetime to a soldier.

Fort Chips had a headquarters building of brick, and a parade ground, and facing it officers' quarters, although since the war there rarely had been more than three officers there and sometimes, as now, only one. There were barracks for the men, stables for their horses, used only in winter, a quartermaster warehouse, guard post, and a deep, square hole in the prairie with beams and canvas over it which was the improvised brig. "If any prisoners want to dig out of that, they got a start, being underground already," Ravalier had said wryly, when he ordered it dug. "But they'll have a long way to go." No one had tried that route for getting out.

On the edge of the reservation, which lay a couple of miles south of the great roadway to Santa Fe and out of sight of it, there was a sprinkling of other establishments, equally important to the men as the fort itself. Favored among them was a lonesome adobe building which everyone knew as Kate Shannon's place, whether they frequented it or not. She, known better as Katydid because whatever a woman could do, she did, was referred to euphemistically in an occasional report as the "laundress," and, in fact, she sometimes did do laundry if the pay was right, although her principal occupation, from which her renown extended, was otherwise. Kate, as all were aware, was an honest woman, realistic with herself, accepting a hard life as her way of getting by, and making the profane best of it, with no remorse about what might have been in the past and no false optimism for the future. Somehow she had stayed off the barreled booze to which so many of her colleagues had become addicted to their ultimate destruction, if their profession didn't ruin them first.

Somehow, too, she had retained that spark of self-pride, a suspicion that some people might have a trifle of good about them, an appreciation for the degrees of evil in herself and others that is the foundation for human dignity. She didn't call it that, of course. Perhaps she had never heard of the expression, nor had most of her steady customers. But in a basic sort of way, Katydid was aware of its existence.

No one knew much of her background, except that it was almost all Army since her late teens. Her first husband had been killed, it was said, after about six weeks of married life, leaving her pregnant, but the baby had died at birth. Her second mate, whom one or two of the old soldiers vaguely had known, was reported to have been a beefy, hairy brute of a noncom, who abandoned Katy and the Army after a year or two of wedded bliss. Since she was not properly divorced and could not take a new husband, and because she had no means and at that time dwelt on the edge of a garrison remote from civilization, she did what was possible and lived with this man or that, meanwhile supplementing her "income," such as it was, by laundering, the only occupation except cooking for some officer and his wife, open to unattached females beyond the frontier. Katy hated to cook. If she disliked the life she led, she detested it to a lesser degree than cooking or playing maid for some overstuffed dame, some officer's wife who, as she sometimes observed, made a living the same way Katy did, but with one man instead of a troop.

Kate was no hypocrite, and had no use for anyone who was.

Despite her hardened shell, she was woman, the only female available to those men of K Company who could not exist without one, or who didn't want to. She had her moments of womanliness, too, of near softness and her heart, which had been hardened by a brutal life on a cruel border, was capable at times of kindness, of generosity toward certain individuals who could not but react with a fierce loyalty and a sort of nameless affection for her.

She had bravely nursed many a man back to health during the cholera epidemic and helped bury some who failed to survive. Katy, although like others of her trade callously demanding payment before the act, knowing full well that if she didn't get the money then she might never see it, had also been known to slip a dollar or so into the pocket of some soldier to last him till payday or buy him a bottle if he really needed one. She was not only the company whore; Katydid also seemed something of a company mascot to many a hard-bitten trooper.

Kate had watched K Company return from its long scout, scanning the column with a practiced eye that told her far more than Captain Ravalier would reveal in his official report. She knew, before talking with any of the men, that they had scouted for a long distance, deducing that from the condition of the pack mules. She knew the outfit had been in a fight, because two men wore bandages still, and that they had won it, because several were mounted on Indian ponies which assuredly had never left Fort Chips with the command. She also was aware that no one had been killed, that none had seen a paymaster, and that she would have to give credit if she expected to do any business, laundry or otherwise. Laundry credit she was not averse to, sometimes, but she tended to draw the line there.

Yet not always.

Joel Vaiking had made it back with the command, but, she noted, he had left as First Sergeant, riding handsomely and competently in the lead with the Captian. Now he was in the ranks and, from her vast Army experience, that could only mean that he had been busted. She could not know why, but she knew he was a man who followed orders and made no trouble, and for those and for personal reasons, she felt that the incident, whatever it was, could not have been his fault. She didn't like Ravalier, anyway. It must have been the Captain who was to blame, she thought primly.

But Joel would tell her himself. He always came to her after a scout. If it was a lucky one, he might stay the night. If it were a brief scout or not much of a success, he would remain only an hour or two, be noncommittal or even morose, hard on her, or at least aloof, and leave without having uttered more than half a dozen words. But this time, when he came, after the 9 P.M. taps, she knew it was different. She could sense it. She opened the door when she heard his step, knowing it from any of the others.

He stood outside the door, looking at her, a blond giant, but so trim and well-proportioned that he appeared to her as the perfection of all men. He had shaved, and somehow that pleased her.

"I'm broke, Kate," he said simply.

"You mean busted," she corrected him, with a half-smile, and not her professional smile, either. "Come on in before someone sees you here after lights out."

She closed the door behind him and stood there, with her back against it, surveying him coolly, yet within her the rising desire Vaiking could always generate just by being there. Despite her rugged life, her breasts were firm and pointed under her robe, and her body, which Joel well knew was suitably soft and yielding, had never grown flabby nor did it yet reveal the wrinkles of age. He drew her to him and kissed her in a preliminary sort of way, hungry with time but not yet with passion.

Why, he *needed* her, she felt, with a start. She experienced a stirring of an emotion she had not known for so very long that she could scarcely even define it. It flustered her.

"Want some coffee?" she asked.

"No. Not now."

Afterward, as they lay side by side in bed, their bodies touching for all their lengths and Joel's arm loosely around her, she asked how he had come to lose his grade. He was silent for a moment.

"I lost it because Ravalier took it away from me," he said flatly. But he wouldn't leave it at that.

"He did it because I listened to his order, understood it, an' refused to carry it out, and I don't know why. I don't know. It was the first time in my life I've ever done that, an' I don't know why."

Joel told her about the order then, so she would understand what he had done, or not done, rather. She reflected on what he had said, then turned toward him and laid her head on his hard chest. "You done right, Joel," she said. "Right. It would of been murder, to of shot her, that way."

Vaiking dissented slightly.

"It would have been soldierin,' to do what the Captain said," he countered. "An' murder or no murder don't enter into it. Somehow, though, I couldn't do it, an' somehow I feel—well, I feel like I don't care I didn't do it. I feel *right* about it, an' that's a damn poor way for a soldier to feel about not carryin' out an order!"

There was no place near the isolated garrison for any sort of amusement or relaxation except Katy's establishment, the sutler's store and the nearby off-reservation sod-walled saloon, and you couldn't patronize any of those joints without cash. So the men, though they grumbled about it, were grateful when Ravalier impatiently ordered the stock to be reshod, equipment worked over, and the outfit retuned to a high state of efficiency should orders come requiring another scout or other action. This took time. Horses and mules did not recuperate as quickly as men, and they would take weeks to come into shape for another hard scout or a good fight. Ravalier so messaged Leavenworth, sending his report and dispatches by courier to Fort Larned, whence they were taken by others eastward, beyond abandoned old Fort Zarah. A dribble of messages came in return, along with routine orders and other official documents, and once even a batch of company mail arrived, all down the same leisurely route.

Only a relatively short time after returning to Fort Chips, therefore, Ravalier heard, with appropriate puzzlement, of the first apparent fruits of his Cimarron adventure: hostiles had swept in on an unsuspecting stage station east of Julesburg and destroyed it, slaying the three men—the hostler and two others—and burning the place to the ground. It might have been an isolated action, of no great significance, except that thereafter hostile and active dog soldiers, fully committed to war, swept up and down the Smoky Hill–Republican stage route, completely disrupting service; raided Julesburg itself and burned down half of it; attacked a number of small emigrant trains, and were reported to have slaughtered what few parties of whites they had run across everywhere on the plains between the Platte and the Arkansas and southwest to the Cimarron. Leaders of the hostiles were reported by survivors to be Dust Devil, Big Ass, and other prominent Cheyennes. A circular letter from Leavenworth demanded from officers at the various posts an assessment of the extent of hostilities and theories as to the reasons for them, known or suspected.

"The Commanding General appreciates the mercurial nature of the Indian," said the letter, in explanation, "and yet that does not seem to fully explain the recent outbreak. It comes so shortly after this very band had indicated it desired to conclude a peace following their hunt, and directly before rations and presents were to be distributed, which the Indians badly wanted, that it seems there might be a further explanation which this headquarters would be eager to possess. Recent action against this band," it continued, with reference to Ravalier's fight, "should have solidified the tendency toward surrender, rather than have postponed it."

Ravalier did not know what other officers at the scattered posts might reply. As for himself, he officially laid the blame for the bloody renewal of plains war upon the "innate deviltry of the Indian nature."

IV

Eight days after K Company's return, its first recruits in three months arrived on foot from the east, herded, harried, hungry. It was a ragged, sullen and suspicious lot of sixteen men. They were lined up on the parade ground to meet Ravalier's initial inspection, almost comical in their ill-fitting blue uniforms with the bright, yellow trim, stiff-billed kepis and their unaccustomed weapons in disordered array. The Captain, irritated because no junior officers had arrived with them for duty at Chips, was in a foul humor. Accompanied by Nero, he could scarcely conceal his distaste for the consignment.

"My God!" he groaned, looking them over. "How long will it take to make soldiers out of them, Nero?"

The First Sergeant caught the officer's mood.

"A lifetime, sir. Some of 'em kin do it in that time," he replied judiciously. "Them others, it might take longer."

One of the recruits directly before Nero, a tall and lean man with a hillbilly face that could only have come from Tennessee, turned his head slightly, while keeping cold, expressionless eyes on Nero, and spat a thick, brown stream of tobacco juice that splattered the ground three inches to the left of the Sergeant's boot. With the grace of a panther Nero jabbed his rifle butt deep into the Tennesseean's

midsection, doubling him up, then brought it in a murderous arc that nailed the recruit behind the ear and cold-
cocked him. Ravalier did not appear to notice.

"You an' you," said Nero evenly, indicating the first two
recruits in line. "Take this stinkin' body to the pit an' toss it
in. Tell the guard this is his number-one prisoner of th' day
and to guard 'im like he was God Almighty 'til he's charged
with disrespect fer an officer, then you two come back here
on th' double. Git!"

He addressed a recruit in the center, a young man named
Harrison with a crisp, clean look about him and some
intelligence in his expression.

"These men had any drillin'?" he demanded.

"No, sir," said Harrison. "We was recruited in—"

"You don't call me 'sir,'" Nero broke in. "Sir's fer
officers such as the Captain, here. Just answer the question."

"We come from all over, I guess. We met at Jefferson
Barracks, an' they held us there two weeks or goin' on
three. But all they did was feed us. They never taught us
nothin'."

"I kin see that," agreed the Sergeant. He turned to the
officer.

"You want I should get someone to drill 'em an' try to
make somethin' besides bowery toughs out of 'em, sir?" he
asked. "Or you want I should shoot 'em an' bury 'em an'
save ourselves all that trouble?"

Ravalier grinned.

"No, don't shoot them, Sergeant. Anyway not today
since it's almost Sunday. Find out what you can of their
backgrounds so we can see what to do with them, and, yes,
get a Corporal to drill them for an hour or two. No extra
detail, though, Sergeant. Just drill them."

"Yes, sir," said Nero, saluting smartly. "We'll just drill
'em."

He pulled a square of paper from a hip pocket and moved

to the first man in line, a short, blocky redhead named Miller, who said he was from southern Illinois.

"What'd you sign up fer?" demanded Nero, a pencil stub poised.

"Figgered the Army'd beat farmin'," said Miller flatly.

The First Sergeant moved slowly down the line, questioning each man and making brief notes on his name, origin, and probable reason for signing up, with any qualifications he might possess. Later he would make a summary and full report for the Captain, who had long since returned to his headquarters office. The reasons for enlistment that Nero wrote down were not always those given him by the recruits. The Sergeant had been in the Army a long time, could read a sign, and generally had a pretty good idea where lay the truth behind a man's statements about his past.

So he calculated three or four of them were farm boys, anxious for a change of scene. Harrison was a former clerk who said he just "had a dose of Army fever, I guess," and whom Nero thought might prove useful at headquarters paper work. Several had past enlistments on their records, and at least one of these, Nero suspected, was a deserter, but it made no difference so long as he answered rollcall for K Company each morning. Three of the recruits were shifty-eyed veterans of misspent lives whom Nero knew had police records somewhere, or ought to have, but, again, it had no significance out here on the plains so long as they soldiered. One of them, who said his name was Hart, obviously had the flux, and maybe malaria, too; he was pale, drawn, weakly, and probably wouldn't last long. Four were foreigners. One was an Irishman who had enlisted to "git somethin' to eat," as he put it. The other three were barely able to speak English, one a German, another French, and the third from some Central European country Nero couldn't spell and had never heard of. The remaining recruits were as varied in origin. A typical bunch, thought the Sergeant, disgustedly. Generally useless now and about sixty percent would still be worthless even after weeks of training. With vast relief he turned them over to a Corporal for drill.

If Nero was openly disgruntled by the batch of K Company recruits, he was no delightful surprise to them, either.

"Is he the best you got?" sourly asked one of Corporal Martin, during the first drilling break. Martin knew whom he meant.

"Nero's First Sergeant," he pointed out curtly. "You do what he says an' don't do nothin' he says don't do, keep your mouths shut, don't cross 'im an' watch yer step when you see 'im, an' likely you'll survive. Don't do thet an' he kin find more ways to remind you than you could ee-magine in a week o' nightmares!"

The new men, lolling about relaxing, listened. They said nothing.

"We had a real fine First Sergeant named Vaiking, but he was too good to last an' got busted by the Captain, so now we got Nero," the Corporal added thoughtfully. "Or Nero's got us. I don't know which."

Kramer, with a face like a ferret and eyes that never rested on anyone or anything for long, looked at Hart, his buddy since Jefferson Barracks, and Hart looked at Woody, whom he had met there also. None said anything, but they reached an unspoken agreement for all of that. It was a way men of their kind had. In the few minutes before supper, they met at a corner of the cook shack.

"I got a bellyful, already," grumbled Woody. Hart, the man who seemed always about to quiver with his persistent malaria, agreed out of the side of his loose mouth: "My belly was full afore I enlisted. It ain't hardly ever been full since," he added, thinking with no deep anticipation of the dry bread and coffee awaiting as the forthcoming supper. His shoulders shook as if he were cold, although the evening was warm enough.

"That guy, Nero. He's the ab-original bastard, I think,"

said Kramer. "Tonight we grab us some horses an' by daylight we'll be halfway east again."

"East, hell," Woody objected. "They'd expect us to go east, all of 'em. I'm fer headin' west, to them minin' camps of Coloraydo. They is lots of money out there, I hear, whether we 'make' it or take it."

"That's a fact," agreed Hart, shivering again. "But we got to get the horses first." He added thoughtfully, "We got to git aroun' that guard, someways, real quiet-like, an' pick good ones, an' saddle 'em up, an' ride to hell out of here, an' do it without gettin' caught, an' do it before midnight, or they'll catch us sure. I don' want to be caught myself, because I already am sick o' th' Army, an' I ain't even been punished for anythin' yet."

Woody indicated Vaiking, standing in the mess line ahead of them waiting for it to move.

"See that yellow-haired son of a bitch over there? He's on stable guard tonight, they tell me."

"He's too big to fight," muttered Hart thinly. "An' if we shoot 'im, that'll waken half the layout. If you kin use a knife, though, you might could do fer him quiet enough."

"Somehow we kin swing 'er," said Kramer. "I never knew I was goin' ter be in the Army so brief a time."

"It seems like a century to me," Woody grumbled. "It seemed like a hundred years already before the recruitin' Sergeant finished givin' me th' oath."

V

Joel Vaiking watched the full moon shoulder out of the east, flooding the plains with a brief moment of ghostly glory, and felt in his bones that this would be a "desertion night," as the noncoms put it.

Desertion was a common enough event in the plains Army of 1867. Like other soldiers, Vaiking had contemplated it himself during his first enlistment. Whether a man deserted depended partly on circumstances and a lot on his officer.

If the officer was brave and at the same time considerate and just, he could be pretty hard on his men without the desertion rate taking off like a flaming arrow. But if he was a coward, or a drunk, or mean-minded, or a queer, or callous, or a brash newcomer out of the Point anxious to exert authority he had not yet earned, desertions from his outfit might be wholesale. Vaiking had heard of companies with rates as high as forty percent a year, and sometimes desertions were so frequent that the company could never maintain its strength and was all but useless until its officers were transferred out and better ones came in. Punishment for the offense was pretty stiff, by the book, but in practice it often was what the officer in command decided it would be—if he could catch the deserter. Sometimes deserters were shot, rather than captured, especially if they were troublemakers or otherwise worthless. Occasionally still they were flogged half to death, although officially flogging went out when the Civil War began.

But punishment might be capricious. It depended upon the man in command, especially if the deserter was caught before his flight became a matter of record, when there would be no need to make explanations to anyone. With an officer like Ravalier, you couldn't predict.

Probably it depended upon his mood. The Captain didn't think much of his job, out here an infinity from established eastern posts where his uniform and dash and spectacular war record amounted to something, particularly with the girls. Here there were no women, unless you counted Indian squaws or Katydid Shannon, and he never considered them at all, except as something to use. Ravalier usually saw only how miserably small his "Army" was, and how vast the plains. He thought, by comparison, of the regimental commands he had held during the war, and once, briefly, a brigade, and the major operations where a man could show his style. If his mind was caught up in reflections such as those, he could be callous and sometimes cruel toward his men, and particularly any who took off without leave and intended to stay as far away as possible until they were recaptured, which they hoped would never occur.

Joel Vaiking was as different from the Captain as toe from heel. He thought of how good what Army there was had to be to do its job on prairies so vast, against enemies so numerous, and he felt it must be wisely managed if it were to do the thing at all. He believed it could. But of course a noncom didn't amount to anything in Army planning, and a private soldier even less, so he kept his thoughts to himself, or believed he did. To the other troopers of K Company, however, they had become apparent long ago.

Vaiking had been hard on deserters and approved of it. You had to be. But he was never vindictive or brutal toward them. He had often found that a man who deserted under the influence of mistreatment and a full moon might be a real brave man, even a hero, in a fight. If treated with justice, no matter how roughly, an erstwhile deserter often later became a good soldier. But he had no great patience with defectors. He was as vigilant to thwart them as he was hard-nosed when he discovered one. And this was a desertion night, if he had ever seen one.

Now he stood silently in the shadows of the adobe corral wall and gripped his rifle closely, and kept his eyes and ears and nose on his job. And he was right.

He felt the approach of the men before he actually saw or heard them. If you kept alert, and adjusted to your job, often you could predict what was coming before it arrived, Vaiking believed. He flattened against the seven-foot wall now. Pressure weighed upon him. He waited. Behind the wall he could hear the muffled stamp of a horse. K Company's stock, usually picketed down near the river of nights, had been brought up with the rise of hostilities. The Captain was taking no chances that blanket-tossing hostiles might stampede away the troop's horses and mules.

Vaiking saw the oncoming men long before they saw him. They dodged quickly across the strip of moonlight between the blacksmith shop and the corral. Joel knew by that they were recruits; no experienced Army man would so expose himself, if he was seriously intent on getting lost. They came out of the moonlight into the depths of the shadows, and before their eyes adjusted Vaiking was among them, slashing out with his rifle butt. He knocked one out, another down, and swung his rifle around as the third started to run.

"Halt where you are," he commanded, "or I'll blow you in half! Come over here and pull your buddies out into the light, so I can get a look."

His voice rang. Woody felt its commanding weight, its dominance over him, its absolute control over him, and for the first time in his brief life he knew the impact of authority, and submitted mindlessly to it. It was the initial act in the making of a soldier.

Under direction he sloshed canteen water in Kramer's face, got him groggily to his feet. Vaiking threw Hart over his shoulder like a sack of oats, directed the other two ahead of him to the pit, and into it, and rolled his burden in behind them. "They can keep Tennessee company," Joel remarked to Martin, corporal of the guard.

"Right, Sarge," agreed Martin, remembering still Vaiking's former grade.

"I best get back," said Joel. "With this moon, they could be more."

The guard record reached Ravalier from Nero with the Morning Report, following his breakfast of salt pork, fried mush and thin stew that came with the monotony of the daily plains breeze. Sometimes there was syrup for the mush, but generally not. Such a breakfast did little for a man, in the way of starting him out for a day in a good frame of mind, but, then, it wasn't supposed to. One thing even the soldiers conceded was that the Captain shared their hard life, with no evasion and no whimpering. As a matter of fact, he didn't care very much about such pleasures as a good breakfast, one way or the other. His mind was on different things. But he had earned a grudging respect with his attitude, whether he intended it or not.

He had Vaiking report in at midmorning. The soldier saluted stiffly and stood at attention.

"At ease, Vaiking, for Christ's sake," said Ravalier wearily. "This ain't West Point."

The big sergeant relaxed.

"You did good work picking up those would-be deserters last night," said the Captain generously. He had completely recovered from his fury of the scouting incident. He usually got over such outbursts quickly. "Nero reminds me we are short of noncoms, like we're short of everything else except neglect. He wants another Corporal to handle those recruits an' whip them into something, if it's humanly possible, which has yet to be proven. We don't have much time to do it, because we are sure to be called out against those hostile idiots before long. You're it."

"Thank you, sir."

Ravalier smiled, as nearly as he could smile without strain.

"Tell Martin to get the prisoners, all four of them, up at 11 o'clock," he directed. "We'll muster the company an' have us a little ceremony. It might do some good, persuade somebody."

Vaiking understood what he meant. He had often seen it: the branding of a captured deserter and his humiliation before the men, a brutal rite designed to impress upon soldiers the notion that it was better to serve than run—or, at least, that it didn't pay to get caught. It was regular Army practice, and everyone was accustomed to it. This occasion proved routine for most of the old soldiers. A fire burned in the center of the parade ground, its acrid cottonwood smoke hazy in the still morning air, the black iron handle sticking out of it and its big "D," for "Deserter," an inch and one-half tall, just beginning to turn pink with the heat from the coals.

The men were mustered, those off-duty. There were fewer than fifty of them, a handful on the vastness of the space all around, almost lost even in the sprawling disorder of Fort Chips, but all the Army there was at this time, in this place. Ravalier formally read a dry statement of the facts, ordered Nero to "Prepare the prisoners for marking!" and Nero ordered Martin and Vaiking to do it. They seized Kramer, the first prisoner, turned him to face the ranks, made him strip off the "uniform he had disgraced," in the words of the Captain, drop the long underwear which was supposed to be white but by now was a dingy gray. He stood there as naked as Adam in the morning, his hairy body curiously animal-like, gleaming in the hot sunlight. Vaiking brought the iron and handed it to Nero, who spat upon the end, the moisture hissing against the hot tip. As Martin and Vaiking held Kramer, Nero planted the iron on his rump, sending out a blast of scorched flesh, a cloud of smoke, and drawing an anguished "Owwww-w-w-w-w!" from the captive. The other two were marked similarly.

"This," pointed out Nero, in high good humor, "is the best place to brand a Cavalryman—he cain't fergit it fer a long time. Whenever he sits down on his saddle, he remembers."

"Take them, all three of 'em, to the shop and have the blacksmith put irons on them, Sergeant," Ravalier directed, as the ceremony ended. "Give them some loads and drill 'em—uh, I'd say, for a week. Make it two."

Nero grinned with anticipation.

"We'd ought to court-martial them and send them to Leavenworth for a few years, an' be done with them," concluded the Captain. "But we need men, any kind of men, too badly. We've got to make do with any rotten material they send us."

"What about him, sir?" asked Nero, jerking a thumb at the Tennesseean, white-faced with lack of food and his time in the pit, but still sullen and bitter. The Captain considered, biting at the long, brown mustache, appraising the prisoner like a mule up for sale, with his quick Cavalryman's glance.

"He never said anything I could hear," said Ravalier. "Can he talk?"

"Say somethin,' soldier!" demanded the Sergeant.

"Ah got nothin' to say," muttered the recruit bitterly.

"Oh, give him some detail, Sergeant," said the Captain, turning away. "Not too much. He needs training, like the others, if he is going to do us any good." He stalked back to the brick headquarters, beating time to some tune in his head with his quirt against his right boot.

Clamping shackles to the prisoners was the blacksmith's job, since no regulation leg irons ever were available. Murphy, the smith, did it as though he was shoeing horses.

To him it was a kindred task. He heated the iron, bent it into the required shape, dipped the hot metal into his tank of sludge to cool it, and clapped it into place, hammering it down and riveting it tight. To each iron was affixed a three-foot length of heavy chain, and attached to its other end was a twenty-pound ball. If a man had traveling to do, he carried the ball. If he needed both hands to work, or eat, or do something else, he dropped the ball to the ground where it remained as sort of a floating anchor.

Sometimes fitting the iron clasp could be excruciatingly painful, if it was too hot, or bent wrong, or of an incorrect size, and once in a while a prisoner's screams of agony could be heard a quarter-mile on a still day. But they never meant anything to Murphy, who stolidly went ahead with his job, paying no more attention to a screaming man than he would to a kicking mule. It didn't take long to do his job, the way he went about it.

The irons for Hart and Kramer went on easily and smoothly, with little apparent discomfort, but Woody complained bitterly.

"Loosen it, Murphy!" he moaned. "For God's sake, the iron is right against my leg-bone. It rubs. I can't wear it that way!"

"Hell you can't, soldier," said Murphy, unconcerned. "That's the way she is in this Army. You want I should take it off, come back when you finish with whatever the Captain give you, an' I'll whack 'er off like you say."

Corporal Vaiking drilled his recruits, or those not in the brig, with his customary thoroughness. He enjoyed the work, although there wasn't much novelty to it, he would be forced to admit. But like thousands of trainees before them, they soon picked up the rudiments of dismounted drill and presented a passable appearance. They were assigned horses then, and he taught them how to care for the animals before they came to equitation lessons. The farm boys took it all in good-humored stride, and those from the cities caught on the sooner because of them.

Daily, whenever he crossed the parade ground, or drill field, as the men called it, he passed the three silent figures, pacing their separate beats, carrying their twenty-pound iron weights, bent under their grotesque packs laden with sixty pounds of stone, back and forth across the flat, their routes beaten hard and shining from their regular, useless, pacing. They said nothing to him, nor he to them. It was routine punishment. Someone always seemed to be undergoing it for some infraction of discipline or regulations. It was Army.

But if he said nothing, his eyes missed nothing, either. On the afternoon of the third day he noticed that Woody's stride seemed more broken than usual. He had limped slightly from the first, and the jerky movement now was more pronounced. It was far worse on the fourth day, and that evening Vaiking fell in beside the recruit as he blindly struggled on with his heavy pack, limping badly, and leaving a trail of bloody tracks.

"Your foot sore?" asked Vaiking, rather needlessly.

"It ain't my foot. It's my goddam leg. This goddam iron! It's like to cuttin' it off!" whimpered Woody.

"Hold on a moment—let me see it," said Joel. He found that the iron shackle had indeed rubbed the shin bare of flesh, with the white of the bone showing through. The shoe was half-filled with blood. The wound was festering, with black encrustations around it, and a spongy swollenness above and below the wound. "You come with me, son," said the Corporal. "Drop your pack here." He helped the recruit struggle out from under the heavy burden of stone. It dropped with a massive thud. Woody limped after Vaiking toward the blacksmith shop, being shut down for the night.

"Hold up, Murphy!" called the Corporal. "Got another job for you."

He indicated the leg-iron.

"Knock this off," he said. "We got to get this man to the hospital."

"Captain's orders?" asked Murphy.

"Hell, he don't know about it, yet, I reckon," said Joel. "But it's got to be done. You can see that."

"I don't take no orders from you, Vaiking. Captain tells me to knock it off, I do it. He don't tell me, I don't do it. Him or Nero."

Vaiking swept up a long-handled pair of hoof nippers, clutched Murphy's shirt-front and swung him against the wall so hard it made the clusters of iron shoes above his head tinkle like bells. He gripped the blacksmith's nose with the nippers and squeezed until Murphy bleated.

"You do like I say or I'll trim your nose like a philanderin' squaw's!" he threatened. "You goin' to do it?"

Murphy nodded. He picked up a sledge and a chisel and in a moment had freed Woody, who sat on the earth floor miserably, gingerly fingering the gaping wound.

"What goes on here?" said Nero's bull-like voice from the doorway.

"We had to knock the iron off Woody's leg as you can see," explained Vaiking evenly. Murphy stood aside, said nothing. Nero looked at the leg, and then surveyed Joel speculatively.

"I didn't hear the Captain give no orders like that," he said ominously. "No one frees no prisoner without the Captain says to do it. Let 'is leg drop off, it don't matter."

"It matters to him," said Vaiking. "It matters to me, too. You go tell the Captain, if you want, but I'm takin' him to the hospital, no matter what you say."

"He don't have to 'go tell the Captain,'" said Ravalier's voice from the gathering darkness. He stepped into the wavering light from the blacksmith's waning fire and glanced quickly at the men clustered there. "What seems to be the trouble, Nero?"

"This is Woody here, the man you give two weeks to, sir," explained the Sergeant righteously. "Vaiking made

Murphy knock off his leg-iron because it scratched his leg. Now he wants to take him to the hospital. I was just goin' to get Murphy to put the iron back on, sir."

The Captain bent over Woody to look more closely at his wound.

"That's a pretty bad leg," he said thoughtfully. "Couldn't you tell the iron was doing that, Sergeant?" Nero looked surprised, then turned swiftly sullen. "I didn't notice it, sir," he said "He was walkin' all right."

"He was limpin' like hell," Vaiking softly countered. "Been doin' it for two days."

The officer straightened, wanting to resolve the business, desiring to support his ranking noncommissioned officer, yet wanting to save Woody, if he could, he needed men so badly.

"Better take him to the hospital and let the doctor look at it, if he is sober enough," he said crisply. "See to it, Nero."

"Yes, sir," muttered the Sergeant. As the Captain disappeared into the darkness Nero looked bleakly at Vaiking. "You take him over there, Corporal," he gritted "An' walk real careful through the night. Every night."

VI

"Indians!" pealed out a man on guard, with a recruit's quivering excitement, fearfulness and stubborn determination all wrapped into his high-pitched voice. "*Indians!*"

It was just a week after Woody had gone to the hospital, from which he had been discharged a day or two before for light duty. Ravalier shouldered past the company clerk and burst through the office door, demanding, "Where? Where? Who said, 'Indians'?" Dipsy Jack, mounted on his knot-headed Cheyenne pony, galloped up from nowhere, plunging to a stop as the guard arrived. The recruit pointed across the river. A mile or two south, hard against the hill, two horseback figures were motionless, in full view of Fort Chopps. The larger was on a spotted horse; the other on a deep bay. They were emblazoned by the rising sun, looking like statues of copper fire against the dull brown of the early autumn plains. They sat there, simply waiting.

Jack squinted from under the black brim of his dusty hat. He spat throughtfully.

"Gin'l," he said then. "It looks like Big Ass an' his woman, but I can't see clear quite so fur. He don't mean no apparent harm, sittin' there like that. I think he wants to talk. You and I should go see fer sure?"

"Yes," breathed Ravalier. "But wait a minute. I'll go with you. Nero! Get me a horse!"

"Yes, sir," said the Sergeant. Instead of sending a soldier he sped himself to the corral, and brought back the Captain's fine-blooded mount, saddled, and one for himself.

"You stay here, Sergeant. Take over in case of—uh—eventualities. Better arm the men and leave some of them here to guard against treachery. Take the rest down along the river and give us what cover you can, though it's so far it won't be much. Keep us in sight, however, as long as you can. Under no circumstances leave that timber and try to join us—understand? Don't do that under *any* circumstances! Keep contact with the post."

"Yes, sir," said Nero.

"Vaiking!" called the officer. "You take Nero's horse here and come along. Keep well behind us, and, in case it's a trap, do what you can to get us out, but don't call on men from the fort, understand?"

"Yes, sir," replied Vaiking, taking the reins of Nero's black horse. The First Sergeant gave him a look to match the color of the animal, resenting that the Corporal should be chosen for this delicate task instead of himself, blind to the need for him to remain. Ravalier, impatient to get underway, caught the suppressed fury of the glance, realized he had hammered the wedge deeper between the two noncoms, but shrugged it off as an exigency of the service, as officers referred to matters of fate which they could not, or would not, bother to change. His action was logical and, to be honest about it, he felt more secure with Vaiking backing him up than he would have with Nero, loyal and obedient though the First Sergeant had always proven himself to be.

The trio rode slowly down to the Arkansas, splashed across it, disappeared momentarily in the screen of timber on the other side, and trotted on, Ravalier and Jack side by side, Vaiking twenty paces or more to the rear, toward the waiting Indians. They had not moved.

"You can't short his guts," said Corporal Martin to no one in particular. He was speaking of the Captain.

"Too bad it ain't Nero with him," grumbled Tennessee, alongside, in his sour twang. "Then ah could lay mah druthers on them Indians."

The scout, the officer and Vaiking rode steadily southward, across the flat sweep of plain, covered with dry, curled buffalo grass, the land rising toward the ravined hills forming the bluffs ahead. They rode warily, their horses' hoofs raising tiny puffs of dust that quickly settled, eyes sweeping the horizon, watching for signs of ambush, knowing the peril of their movement, yet having no choice. Big Ass watched them come, he and his woman, the manes and tails of their horses floating gracefully in the early breeze, but the animals silent and wooden as their riders.

"He got his woman along to show he don't mean war," muttered Jack, as they rode on. "It's their way. Sometimes they mean what they seem to mean, an' sometimes they don't. I hope today he means it, but we best take no chances we don't have to take."

They stopped one hundred and fifty yards from the savages.

Jack raised his rifle overhead, and brought it down athwart the pommel. Big Ass raised his lance, and lowered it. He and the woman stepped their horses half the distance to the white men, and halted them again. No one yet had spoken.

The Indian broke the silence, speaking a guttural sentence.

"He say he wants to talk," interpreted Jack.

"That's what we came out for," said Ravalier unsmilingly, his eyes part of the time on Big Ass, but flicking away from the Indian to sweep the broken hills a few hundred yards behind the two of them. "Ask him if he wants to talk about peace or war."

An interchange followed.

"He say peace," said Jack. "I don't trust the son of a bitch, though."

"Ask him who he's speaking for, himself or his people," demanded the officer.

Another broken conversation.

"He say his people want peace, too. They is tired of war, he say. He said his people want to come to the fort to talk with the great officer, an' I suppose he means you, but he don't say. What'll I tell him?"

"Invite him in to the fort today, now. Maybe we can use him for a hostage or something. Offer him whiskey, if he comes in, an' presents for his woman—ain't she ugly? See if you can get him to come in with us."

Jack interpreted. Big Ass shook his head, motioned back toward the hills, and fell silent.

"He say he cannot do that because his brothers back beyond the hills are anxiously awaiting his word," explained Dipsy Jack. "He say he would like to sit down here, on the ground, off our hosses, an' smoke with us to show his good faith which I don't believe fer a minute he got any of. Mebbe he just wants to get us off our hosses."

"Tell him we smoke when we talk peace, not in the middle of war," replied Ravalier shortly. During the conversation the two parties had edged closer together until now only twenty-five yards separated them. As Jack translated Ravalier's final comment, the Indian broke. The woman jumped her horse toward the Captain's. She reached out for his bridle reins, close to the bit, and missed only by inches. The buck screamed a high-pitched war cry. The ravines behind him appeared to open and flush out torrents of mounted warriors from concealment within the defiles. Dipsy Jack swung his rifle and bludgeoned the squaw off her horse while Ravalier wheeled just as Big Ass hurled his lance toward him. The Captain's movement saved his life, but the feathers on the tip of the weapon slapped his face as it whipped by, so close was it to his body. The two of them whirled their horses and spurred for the post, just as Vaiking swept by them, toward the enemy.

"Vaiking!" shouted the officer over his shoulder. "Vaiking! For God's sake that's half the Cheyenne nation! Come on! Come on! Back to the fort!"

But Vaiking paid no heed, having eyes only for Big Ass who, having flung his lance, now was weaponless, seeking to spin his pony back toward the oncoming warriors. Vaiking cut him off, with the enemy only two or three hundred yards distant and coming on at a mad gallop. He brought his pistol down witih crushing force against the Indian's skull, stunning him. Then, holding the swaying body to his horse, Vaiking wrapped the pony's jaw rope around his wrist, holding its head up close to his McClellan, sank spurs deep into his mighty black horse, and literally towed the unconscious Indian, pony and all, at a pounding run back toward the river.

If the spotted pony had stumbled, or his own horse had tripped, he would never have made it, but they kept their feet and though the warriors gained slowly on him, Vaiking brought his prisoner in a thundering rush to within the long-range cover of Nero's men, under the timber, before he could be brought down.

Under protection of the guns along the timber, Ravalier and Dipsy Jack had jerked their mounts to a halt, swung out of the saddles and stared back at the oncoming Vaiking and his prisoner. He brought his two horses scampering in among the trees and hauled them to a jolting stop. Jack was speechless and the Captain nearly so, but his wide grin indicated he appreciated the soldier's quickness of thought and action.

"Good work, Vaiking, great work!" he cried, ungrudgingly. "We can use him."

"Hope so, sir," smiled Vaiking. "You want I should lock him up someplace?"

"You bet. Take him into the post and put him in the orderly room under a heavy guard. Tell Nero I said to guard

him with his very life. Better have the surgeon look at his
head an' make sure you didn't bust his skull."

"Yes, sir," said Vaiking, turning the two horses toward
the river. "I think it's too thick to've been cracked by one
little ol' smack."

He forded the shallow river with the two horses, still
holding the swaying body of the groggy Indian upright, and
turned the prisoner over to Nero with the Captain's
instructions.

"I'll guard the fat bastard all right," growled the First
Sergeant. "Give me my horse before you go back to bein' a
hero an' git him killed." He was jealous anew at the
soldier's feat which, Joel felt, had done nothing to close the
breach between them. He turned the sweating horse over to
the Sergeant and joined the thin line of blue-clad troopers
maintaining a desultory fire against the Indians, who had
halted so far distant as to be almost beyond range. Vaiking
stopped the shooting.

"Don't waste the ammunition," he advised. "They don't
know what to do with Big Ass gone and so many armed
men facing them. They'll never attack now."

He was right. By afternoon the volatile enemy had sifted
back into the hills, and by evening the post was silent and as
alone on the prairie as it had seemed at dawn to be. Ravalier
brought in the men from across the river. With Jack he met
Nero and Vaiking at the orderly room, where the prisoner
was being held.

The big Indian, still with dried blood on the side of his
face, was morosely defiant. Jack talked with him briefly, but
he kept shaking his head. No doubt he expected to be shot,
but, in any event, he was not talking.

"Ask him where his people are camped," Ravalier
suggested as a starter. Big Ass shook his head and said
nothing.

"Mebbe he wants to be treated nicer, like to have some
whiskey," suggested Jack, disgustedly.

"Whiskey, hell. Ask him—wait a minute. Doctor, you
got any castor oil or anythin' that works like that?"

demanded Ravalier. The surgeon, a bleary-eyed veteran of numerous campaigns and countless bouts with more bottles than he or anyone in the Army could recall, puzzled deeply and thought he had, or at least he used to have some. Ravalier sent the orderly to his own quarters for half a bottle of whiskey, and the surgeon to rummage around through his stores for the castor oil. He told him to fill the whiskey bottle the rest of the way with the medicine, and "shake it up well. I hope they mix!" Then he had the treated bottle brought to the prisoner.

The Indian's eyes opened at the sight of it, and a tiny smile played at the edge of his mouth.

"He called Big Ass because he got one," muttered Nero approvingly. "Let him use it."

Ravalier ingratiatingly offered the doctored bottle to the Indian, who snatched it greedily. The officer ordered him taken to an abandoned building for safekeeping, and the Indian stalked off, clutching the bottle with a death grip.

"By mornin' he'd ought to be weak enough so we can carry on our conversation!" Ravalier grinned. Nero considered it a great joke. Vaiking and Jack said nothing. There was nothing to say. Such matters, involving Indians, were limited only by the ingenuity of the men involved. They were a commonplace, a part of soldiering. Not worth comment. Thought, either.

As Corporal of the guard next day, Vaiking attended the fresh interrogation. The doctored whiskey had done its work well, judging from the Indian's appearance, and that of his "cell." Big Ass, who had gulped down most of the contents of the bottle, suffered not only from a hangover, but reeled with weakness, held his stomach, and his eyes rolled. He was as miserable a human being as Joel ever recalled. Yet, the big noncom knew, if the warrior were offered another bottle today, right now, he would snatch at it, so addicted was he, like most Indians, to whiskey or liquor of any sort; so little did they comprehend what it did to them.

Perhaps his hangover was too thick still for him to realize that the bottle had been "poisoned." Maybe he knew and didn't care. It held whiskey.

"Man he sure stinks, don't he?" marveled Ravalier at no one in particular. "Jack, ask him again where his people camp."

The scout put the Captain's question into guttural syllables. Big Ass listened carefully, an owlish expression flushed his face, he winced from some interior pang, but his great body heaved and rolled with amusement. He was still drunk, but not so drunk he didn't know what was said or where he was. He shook his head.

"He say who can tell?" translated Dipsy Jack. "They go where the buffalo go, an' the buffalo go with the wind an' grass. He tellin' th' truth, there."

Ravalier pursed his lips and considered briefly.

"Ask him how many clans are on the warpath," he demanded. The guttural interchange followed.

"Now he gettin' stubborn," reported Jack. "He say his clan, the Dog Soldiers, fight, but he don't say nothin' about any of th' others. Don't think he will, neither, in his present frame of mind."

"Ask him about the Bowstrings, the Lances, the Red Shields, the Kit-foxes," urged Ravalier thoughtfully. "If we knew which societies were out, we could better operate against 'em, if we had the means to operate at all. Besides, it would make my report look good, if I could find out."

Jack turned to Big Ass, who rested his face in his hands, stared morosely, and reeled as waves of illness apparently swept over him. The Indian's opaque eyes were on Jack's face as the scout talked, but when he finished he shook his head once more, and replied deep from within his tortured throat.

"He say he don' know. He a Dog Soldier, an' they is out, but he not a Bowstring, a Lance, a Red Shield or a Kit-fox, an' how would he know if they is out? He's lyin', o' course."

"Of course," agreed Ravalier. He surveyed the quivering hulk of the Indian with apparent distaste.

"Maybe he needs his memory jarred a little," he mused. "Vaiking, take over."

The Corporal found the order not unexpected. He had carried out what had to be done on other occasions, to hapless prisoners, and never felt even a twinge of conscience. That was before he started to think, however, come to consider it. He stepped toward the miserable war leader, clutched a fistful of his long, lousy hair with his left hand and hoisted Big Ass to his feet, backhanded him across the mouth and pinned him to the brick wall. He cocked his right fist to bury it in the warrior's great belly. The Indian's eyes, suddenly sober, stared into his—cold, defiant, hating, unafraid, knowing from somewhere what was to happen to him, and daring the white giant to do his worst, aware that there was no hope of mercy, that he was a prisoner among a horde of enemies, that there could be no escape, yet not quavering; expecting, waiting, helpless, yet indomitable; a prisoner, yet somehow free. All of this was in his staring eyes, as Vaiking drew back his great fist. His arm shook with sudden indecision.

"Go on, Corporal, for Christ's sake slug him a few times," urged Ravalier.

"I—can't, sir," hoarsely whispered Vaiking. "As God is my witness, I can't do it. I'm sorry, Captain. I cannot do it. I don't know why."

Silence as thick as the heavy walls spread over the room.

"Didn't I hear you say that once before, not long ago?" demanded the officer harshly.

"You did, sir," agreed the noncom, turning a taut and twisted face toward his superior. "I didn't know why then, an' I don't know why now. I couldn't do it then; I can't do it now."

Ravalier stared at Vaiking, a little ridge of uncertainty and puzzlement rising between his odd eyes.

"What the hell am I goin' to do with you, Corporal?" he

wondered. He slowly wagged his head. "You're the best damn combat soldier in th' company, an' the worst at taking an order when your mind goes against it. Goddam it, I busted you once, and here that didn't do any good." Again he shook his head. Big Ass for the moment was forgotten. The Indian again was sitting on the wooden stool, his face in his hands, staring at nothing.

"Well," decided the Captain, with a noisy sigh. "Go to the everlastin' pit an' slide in! And on the way, tell Nero to report here. Nero don't think. When I tell *him* to do something, he can take an order. That's why he's First Sergeant instead of you." The Captain turned away, adding, almost under his breath, "About the only reason."

VII

Joel Vaiking had often booted erring soldiers into the pit, but he had never been in it himself, and it had been dug long before he arrived at the post.

The hole was eighteen by eighteen feet square, and sixteen feet deep, and was roofed with tent canvas over a wooden frame. On good days the canvas sides were rolled up a foot or two to let in light. During the violent summer thunderstorms, for which this part of the plains was justly famed, some rain inevitably soaked in, making the packed earth floor a slimy mess, and there always was the chance that a cyclone would seep through, taking the roof to hell and gone forever. When that day came, any man sentenced to the pit, and actually in it, would be safe enough from the wind, but he might be drowned. If such a lamentable event should happen while Ravalier was commanding officer, the victim could count on but little sympathy of course, since the Captain believed no man ever entered the pit who did not abundantly deserve all its discomforts, risks and dangers.

When a man dropped into it, he brought along his own blanket and mess gear, was furnished a bucket and a canteen of water daily, if the guards thought of it and got around to it. Food, or what passed for food, was brought to him twice a day unless he had a working assignment, or punishment "outside," when he was held at the mess hall to eat.

Naturally no man ever was confined to the pit for very long. A couple of weeks was about the maximum. And no inspecting officer from other posts had ever complained about it, or reported adversely on it, because none had ever seen it, or knew it was there, or, for that matter, had ever expressed an interest in the punishment of prisoners. The poot Civil War frontier Army had other things to be concerned about besides ill-treatment of prisoners, and of course no victim had ever complained to higher authority because there was no mechanism for him to do so, and he probably would not, even if there had been. Morale, health and efficiency were terms not yet concocted, and so long as there were a sufficient number of men ready for duty to fulfill its mission in at least a minimum way, superior officers were content. Anything more was a pleasant surprise and subject for congratulations up and down the chains of command.

Corporal Vaiking had but two other "cellmates," Hart and Kramer, who jangled in with their rattling leg irons following retreat, about sundown, and clattered out shortly after dawn to begin again their monotonous, useless daylong march under their sixty-pound loads of stone, back and forth across the parade ground, along the paths they had worn smooth, following the courses of other prisoners before them. They were in the final days of their "sentence," and on their sketchy food they were exhausted when they reached the pit at night. Hart said no word. Kramer cursed feebly and unimpressively. They rolled up in their sodden blankets against the mud walls, and somehow slept until dawn.

Vaiking wished he had some duty to do, for his powerful body craved activity, but he had none. He was not a foul-up, against whom most of the ingenious tortures devised by Army captors to needle captives were made to operate. He was there simply for disobeying an order, for being unable to obey, as he believed. His long training taught him that his confinement was just, that Ravalier had no choice but to order it, though the search for reasons behind his disobedience tortured his mind.

He scarcely noted that he had nothing to eat the first night, until Riley, on guard, told him in the morning that Nero had intercepted him with the food, and taken it away. "He says, 'beginnin' prisoners don't eat,' just like the bastard wanted to starve you to death," the Irishman explained from the head of the slide into the pit.

"Aw, he just wants to lever his own weight into the sentence," growled Vaiking. "It'll pass." He ate the hard, dry biscuits and drank the canteen cup of coffee that Riley had brought him, and grinned up at the soldier. "One fine meal a day like this ought to do a man who's not on duty," he said.

Again that night there was no supper for him. Vaiking was glad when Hart and Kramer rattled in, and huddled in their blankets against the dirt walls in the twilight. Hart's face appeared flushed, even in the dim light, but Kramer was talkative, now that his sentence was about at an end. "We been in this rotten cave almost two weeks now," he confided.

"You'd ought to get out about Saturday, I guess," Vaiking thought.

"What they got you in for—you try to take off, too?" demanded Kramer.

Vaiking laughed shortly. "Worse than that," he admitted. "The Captain tol' me to do something, an' I wouldn't do it. They ain't no worse crime in the Army, not even deserting."

"I'm glad they is someone blacker than us," muttered Kramer, trying to settle into his corner. "I was beginnin' to think we was th' worst the Army had ever heard of."

Hart, who still had said nothing, huddled against the wall, staring glassy-eyed at the floor, and now began to quiver and, in a few moments, to shake more and more violently.

"He's got the ague," explained Kramer, unconcerned. "Come into th' Army with it. Sometimes it passes soon. Other times it lasts most of th' night. But it's always passed, so far. This hell-hole is so damp it don't help, though."

Vaiking got up and laid his own blanket over Hart, who appeared not to notice.

"I don't think he's really cold at such times," speculated Kramer. "He just shakes is all."

"Looks cold to me," said Vaiking. He watched Hart, whose eyes had begun to roll as his gyrations increased. "He's really sick, that one."

The Corporal looked up the ramp and called, "Guard! Guard!"

Riley's face appeared in a few minutes.

"We got us a pretty sick man down here, Riley," said Vaiking. "He'd ought to go to the hospital. Tonight."

"I'll ask Nero," said Riley, disappearing hastily. He was back in ten minutes. "The Sergeant says he'll keep till mornin' is what he says," explained the soldier glumly. "I can't let 'im out without Nero or the Captain says so."

"Go tell Ravalier, then, Riley, but hurry, for God's sake," urged Vaiking. Once more the soldier disappeared, and again returned in a few minutes.

"The Captain's drunk," he reported. "He tol' me to see Nero. I went to Nero again an' he tol' me to get th' hell out and go back on guard an' he'd take care of lettin' any prisoners out. They ain't nothin' else I kin do, Joel. I wisht there was, but there ain't."

Hart didn't moan. He said nothing. He huddled in the two blankets and shook, more violently than even the pronounced shivering, and the spasms increased minute by minute. Vaiking felt his head, and it was cold. "Sometimes he's burnin' up, and then he's cold," said Kramer, indifferently. "Seems like he can't make up his mind. Sure glad it ain't me." He wrestled around to get off of his branded rump, and fell asleep.

Before midnight Hart's shaking abruptly ceased. He lay so still Vaiking examined him once more. He was dead. Vaiking took his own blanket back and pulled the other up over Hart's face.

He had realized vaguely, when the sickly Hart showed up with the other recruits, that he was virtually a goner, that he couldn't live very long, but this was a hell of a way to die. Vaiking settled down across the pit, his back against the mud wall, his arms folded across his drawn-up knees, and his chin on them. It would have been blacker than sin on the floor of the pit but for a dim light diffused through the canvas roof from a half-moon. With his eyes accustomed to the gloom he could make out Hart's still form, and could hear Kramer's snoring. The place smelled mouldy and rotten.

His mind turned his Army career over and over, inspecting, examining, and assessing it.

For the first time in his whole young life, he wondered specifically, "Why?"

Why did there have to be authority in the Army? He knew the answer because he had been a soldier for many years. But what about blind authority, *stupid* authority? Joel was loyal to the Army. He realized that while usually its authority was just, sometimes it was not. Being channeled through human beings, some intelligent and compassionate, others brainless or cruel, authority would naturally be exercised variously. He didn't have to name names. He knew lots of examples of the one or the other. You could always find them.

Why, then, did a man have to obey? Authority itself was the big thing. If you didn't have authority, you would have anarchy, or chaos, or both. You had to obey even stupid authority, because authority itself was good and necessary.

But what if, sometimes, a man *could not* obey authority, like these times when he was ordered to do something and found himself unable to carry out the commands? He realized that the times when he hadn't obeyed was because the order was to brutalize someone, or do something so cruel that it conflicted with his vaguely defined sense of justice, which the Army had never been able to wipe out entirely. But that was arguing beside the point, he felt. Or was it? Maybe that was the whole point.

That was authority, and he was a soldier, and he knew that by Army standards he had been wrong. But he was a man, too, and he had his own way of looking at things. He, soldier or not, authority or no, could not overcome the man in him, and whatever made up a man, and shoot that squaw or beat up that Indian. He felt he was wrong, and he blamed himself alone, but he also was aware that if he were faced with those things again, he still wouldn't do them. Because he could not clearly see where the authority of the Army ought to stop and that of a man begin, he felt unsure, as though he was wrestling with shadows, and it worried him. He wasn't used to worry. A sharp, decisive man, he wanted things plain and clear-cut so he would know what to do and not have to make crisp decisions on hazy information. Vaiking had no way of knowing it, but he held this complaint in common with most thinking men; it was a sign of his mental growing up, of maturing.

But if, in cases like these, he thought, a man could not obey authority, just because he was a man—what then?

Authority, he knew damned well, could not be watered down to fit occasions like these. More likely a man would have to do what he could and smash himself against it because one man cannot change it, and probably should not, even though he couldn't live with it. If things ever worked up to a crisis, what would be the result? Would a man just have to wreck himself, amount to nothing, disappear with no concrete result whatever? Vaiking didn't know. Nor do most men. It is usually a case of working things out as you come to them; that is the best way, the only way, since no man can prepare himself at all points for a future he cannot predict. Being a soldier, Vaiking had accepted the tenet that the Army was more important than the man, but he recognized that this was merely evading the answer, because it did not explain what a man was to do when he could not accept his submissive role.

Funny how you could wrestle with such thoughts in the blackness of deep night. Probably it was because he was hungry, and his stomach was working on his brain, or something. You rarely came to clear conclusions, at times like these, on an empty stomach, or anyway to conclusions you could remember clearly afterward. It was a thing to fret about, though, and so he thought himself into a troubled sleep.

Kramer was taken back to his endless rounds come morning and later on they carried Hart out, taking him to the graveyard. Vaiking wondered idly if they took the shackles off before they buried him. If Nero thought they'd use them again soon, they probably did. It made no difference to Hart, or to anyone else now. Vaiking was sure getting hungry, not that he was doing any work, but just from habit, he was sure. He would be damned if he would say anything, though. That's probably what Nero wanted—him to say something, ask for chow, or even beg for it. He'd starve, first. Nero would see he wouldn't starve, though. You couldn't hardly starve in one week. But you could sure get hungry.

In late afternoon, however, he got food, good food, and a lot of it. The guard let Kate Shannon come to the head of the ramp and talk down it to him, and he found that she had sent the grub. Wolfing it hungrily, he could not still his curiosity.

"How'd you know I could use it? How did you get this past Nero, Kate?" he quizzed gratefully.

She shrugged her shoulders.

"Riley told me they wasn't feedin' you," she replied indifferently. "Figured you'd be hungry by now."

"You was right," Vaiking agreed. "Did Nero bust a leg or somethin', that he let you bring it?"

"He let me," she said. Then she added, matter of factly:

"Nero got what he wanted. You get what you want, which is food, and I get what I want. Everyone's satisfied."

Vaiking understood her implication, but he went on eating, anyway.

"What do you want, Kate?" he wondered.

"Well," she said, "right now I want for you to come out of that pit as healthy as you went into it. I don't want you starved, Joel."

VIII

Fort Arnold Chopps lay out of sight, but within a couple of miles of the busy Santa Fe Trail, slicing diagonally across the plains from Westport Landing. Most of the trail crossed the Arkansas a hundred or hundred and fifty miles southwest of the post. The big reason, or the only one, in the view of some of the boys, for establishment of the outpost in the first place had been to protect the traffic on the trail. That was not entirely true, of course, but so some of the soldiers grumbled: that they were governmental tools ordered to risk their necks almost daily in defense of private businessmen and their operations. It made a soldier feel better to complain on the basis of such theories.

No Indian war, no terror of the plains, could halt the steady stream of caravans rocking and swaying down the trail from the States, nor the ceaseless return of parties, sometimes of horsemen alone, or riders driving mules or other portable wealth back to Missouri and the Mississippi River communities. These companies, coming and going, kept to the road which ran on the high ground north of the fort, and Army units rarely had any direct contact with any of them unless an escort were needed for a stated distance. This was the case only when they were carrying freight of high value and great portability, or when the Indian menace was acute, or in case the owner or wagonmaster knew some Senator or other powerful Washington figure whose favor the Army wanted, or needed to cultivate, or some kindred reason. Such instances did not happen frequently, sometimes only once or twice a season, or even less. There was little movement along the trail from November to March, because then the grass was poor and livestock could not maintain its strength. It was heaviest from May through September. Sometimes a couple of trains a day would rumble through, mostly going west. Often the wagons were sold or broken up at Sante Fe, or even Chihuahua, and the wagoners and train crews returned more swiftly, mounted on purchased horses or mules which could be readily sold at a fresh profit in the States. No man who had captained wagons all the way to Chihuahua ever desired to bring them back to the States again. Once over that route was enough.

The courier who slipped his jaded horse into the fort just before dawn of the fourth day after Vaiking had been sentenced to the pit, could combine two or more of the required specifications in his urgent request for an escort. For one thing, he was with a small, fast train of mules and six light wagons, reversing the usual order and going back to the settlements from Santa Fe, loaded with gold from southwestern mines, and similar freight. But, more importantly, the caravan brought along the most intense concern of the venerable governor of New Mexico in the person of his lovely and wayward daughter, whom he devoutly hoped, after she had seen the wonders and delights of St. Louis, would remain in the States until his present appointment to office had run out and he could join her at his ancestral home in Kentucky. She had caused quite enough turmoil in New Mexico.

He was not too confident that his fervent wishes would bear fruit, however.

The messenger was taken to Ravalier, who instantly caught the implications of the problem, and its possibly remote but nonetheless real possibilities for his own career perhaps, and approved dispatch of an escort to see the train as far east as Larned, or through the worst of the Indian-ravaged country. He could not send First Sergeant Nero with the small escort, because Nero was required to fulfill post duties that the Captain himself otherwise would have to undertake. Besides, in a case like this, there was no one in whom he had greater confidence than Vaiking, so he ordered him brought out of the punishment dungeon to the headquarters building. With four or five days' stubble on his thinned face, and his clothing crumpled as though it had been slept in for most of a week—as, indeed, it had—Vaiking looked anything but a responsible soldier for an important mission. But Ravalier knew his man well.

"Corporal, shave, take a bath and clean up," said the Captain. "You will go with a detail of eight men to the Cimarron Crossing, one hundred and thirty-five miles up the Arkansas. There is a small train waiting there, pointing east. You will escort this train to the vicinity of Larned and turn it over to a suitable military escort from there, for which I will give you a written request. Go to the Cimarron crossing with Dipsy Jack and a Mr. Blanton, who came in this morning. Understood?"

"Yes, sir," said Vaiking, glad to be out of the pit and, like any soldier, delighted with an assignment which would offer an opportunity for a change of scene. But more than that, the duty would serve perhaps to quiet the restless searching of his mind, and possibly still the strange doubts that had shaken him during his long hours in confinement. Perhaps he might discover answers out there. Even Vaiking, with all his experience, however, could not foresee the perilous nature of his mission, and that its risks were not from Indians.

"Don't forget the bath," said the Captain again. "You smell like hell. I understand there is a young woman with this train, the daughter of Governor Raggensworth, who is going east, and we wouldn't want her to get the wrong idea of what soldiers on the plains normally smell like."

"Yes, sir," agreed the Corporal, accustomed to the Captain's hangover humor.

"Nero will assign the men to go with you," continued Ravalier, more conversationally, shuffling papers on his desk. He added, "This is an important duty. If you don't want any of 'em, see me." It was a novelty for an officer to suggest thus interceding between two of his noncommissioned officers, but Ravalier was concerned that this duty be handled smoothly, that the detail be fulfilled without any preventable incident. That was the main reason why he had picked Vaiking to head it. The Corporal might disobey bizarre orders, and have to be punished for it, but he was reliable, and he was intelligent, and he had good judgment.

"I understand," the Captain concluded, "that a wagon broke down and had to be fixed where they are now camped, which is a strong position. But the real reason they are not proceeding as planned is because of the Cheyenne trouble, on the one hand, and that a considerable portion of their personnel returned to Santa Fe, in a sort of—ah—mutiny, the way it was reported to me. It is said that this mutiny was caused in some manner by the young woman. I tell you this only for your information. My order is that you use tact and judgment but somehow get the damned train with its—ah—politically important cargo and—ah—personnel, to hell out of my district without a catastrophe of *any sort*. Understand?"

"Yes, sir," said Vaiking, not truly comprehending at all.

At dusk on the third day of a hard and rapid march, the escort, with Jack and Blanton, filed down the long grade to the line of smoky cottonwoods marking the course of the Arkansas, the deeply grooved trail leading directly to a sandy ford, lost in the gathering evening. The train was parked in a V-shaped defensive position, hard against a high cutbank where, if the stock were driven into its shelter, it would be impossible for hostiles to make away with the animals. Whoever planned this arrangement knew well what he was doing, Vaiking thought approvingly, as he led his men to the only opening into the small park. A rangy individual with a sardonic expression on his Texas face, awaited them, bearing a rifle across his arm.

"You made good time, soldier," he greeted the noncom. "Wasn't really expectin' you 'til tomorrow."

"We rode fast," Vaiking agreed.

"Name's Tucker," said the Texan. "Lafe Tucker. Train commander."

Vaiking introduced himself and Jack.

"Any of your boys kin drive teams?" demanded Tucker hopefully. Joel guessed that some of them could, in a pinch.

"Good enough," responded the Texan. "That's what we need mostly, is teamsters, though with the Cheyennes out it won't do no harm to be as strong as we kin. But mainly we want to git to Westport as soon as may be, an' with mules that oughter be pretty prompt. They is all in pretty fair shape, still. The rest didn't do 'em no harm."

Vaiking accepted a cup of coffee at Lafe's smouldering campfire.

Tucker drank his swiftly, draining the grounds over the coals.

"Yeah," he grunted. "It's what comes of havin' a unattached, good-lookin' female along that can't stop rovin', by eye, or by temperament, or by foot. We'd hardly left Santa Fee when she had one teamster agin another, an' by the time we got to here there'd been one gun fight with a man wounded, an' wagon set agin wagon. Hell of a mess. I couldn't stand th' bellerin' an' fightin' finally, an' sent a passel of 'em back to Santa Fee, an' thet's why we needed you fellers. Thet's why I want to git to Westport as soon as ever we kin an' git shet of this train fer once an' all. I was a damn fool fer takin' it, though th' pay is good."

"Did I hear someone mention me?" demanded a low, penetrating, woman's voice from behind the soldier.

"Good God," moaned Lafe. "This is Corporal Vaiking, Miss Kim Raggensworth," he said, stressing the word

"Corporal," although he knew it wouldn't do any good. "Governor's girl," he added, without much hope there, either.

Kim was almost twenty. She had a towering mass of red hair above a face that was regular, eyes that were brown, a mouth that was full, and body more than adequate in conformation, Vaiking saw at a glance. For some reason warning bells jangled through his mind, and he hazily recalled the Captain's caution against disaster. He was beginning to understand, but his resistance was to be savagely battered, he instinctively felt.

As a matter of record, Vaiking held out for three days and almost four nights. His was a fairly firm resistance, considering the concentrated nature of the attack. The more he stood off, however, the more determined the assault upon his defenses, Kim becoming more and more intrigued by the apparent aloofness of the tall soldier, until finally she overwhelmed him. Once having surrendered, Vaiking was happy and accepted his fate with a large dose of equanimity. He had bedded down under a wagon as usual, the train that night being less than twenty miles from Chips, and four days from Larned. His blankets were somewhat separated from those of the other men. When Kim rushed to him in the post-midnight gloom with that most ancient of yarns about having been "frightened" from her own wagon-quarters, Joel silently lifted the cover. She slipped in beside him, and he embraced her hungrily, neither saying another word until toward morning when she left for her wagon before the guard's awakening call could set the camp stirring. It had been a completely satisfactory night, for Vaiking. It was routine for Kim, but, blinded by male vanity, the Corporal could not be aware of that.

He had found in the adventure a substantial reinforcement of confidence in his masculinity; so men always profit from the sex act. For the first time in long weeks he felt sure of himself, confident, his own man completely once more. He was quietly exultant as he pulled on his rough cowhide soldier-shoes after the guard's call, and he felt possessive about Kim and attracted to her. Against all the evidence, including that of his own common sense, he felt like a conqueror this morning, rather than the conquered, as in fact he had been, and for him there were just the two of them: himself, a man once again, and the beautiful, red-haired, passionate Kim Raggensworth.

She, busy behind the drawn canvas of her private wagon, felt far differently, of course, woman that she was and odd little character that she had become.

Kim was unlike most of her sex, who discover in intercourse a deep attachment for their partner, whoever he might be, and, more often than not, a considerable emotional involvement.

Kim had had an unusual experience to start off her brief sex life. In common with many redheads, she had been afflicted from puberty with what the folks then called "woman trouble," but in her case it was cruelly aggravated. Because of the wealth and influence of her family, the physician had been able to arrange for her to enter a Kentucky hospital for what he called a "hysterectomy," an operation not common in that day, although, he assured her, its principle had been learned "hundreds and hundreds of years ago." Until fairly recently, however, mortality following the operation was so high that it was rarely performed. About 1850, however, this one particular hospital began having far greater success with it, for reasons not then entirely clear, though later realized to have been because of its insistence upon soap and sanitation. Although the waiting list was long, Kim's family influence secured her a place. The operation was a complete success, the mental adjustment afterward less so. But the operation freed her not only from her intolerable woman's pains, but from the fears and inhibitions which normally sharply limited sexual promiscuity in that day. Not only that, but because of the operation, which did not interfere in any way with the sex drive but only with its predictable results, Kim appeared to feel herself somehow incomplete, and seemed driven to overuse of sex to prove herself truly a woman.

She discovered a masculine sort of conquest-awareness, and turned from one affair to another with little sense of involvement, suspending scalps from her belt, as it were, as a decoration for her vanity. It was as though the operation, crude though it was, had left her oversexed. If she had ever analyzed it, which of course she could not, and would not, do, she might have realized that sex was sort of a compensation for her irretrievably lost womanhood. Instead she thoughtlessly pursued her blithe way, her singular career, quite unconcerned about the wagon trains she wrecked, the men she disillusioned, the evil, and sometimes the good, she wrought.

Kim Raggensworth found sex, freed from worries over possible results, an endless game, and she would play it with virtually anyone. She had progressed beyond various teamsters to Corporal Vaiking, and now she was to try her luck with a commissioned officer; for that day, in late morning, Captain Ravalier with a two-man escort, met the train while ostensibly hunting buffalo or, perhaps, Indians. In point of fact, his curiosity had overcome his not very extensively developed scruples. He had forgotten his own dictum to Vaiking against any "catastrophe." He had, to put it briefly, come out to see for himself this paragon of womanly dissension who had toyed with his imagination in absentia ever since the plaintive call for help had been received by messenger from Lafe Tucker, when he was backed against a river cutbank without enough men left to move his train.

The Captain rode up the length of the outfit, a handsome, lean figure on his personal horse, said to be half-thorough-bred. Kim, through the drawstring opening at the rear of her wagon, which was second in line, speculatively observed his progress. She liked the tallness, the slenderness of him, the set of his shoulders, his sweeping mustaches, the arrogance with which he surveyed the train as he rode alongside it. Here, she reflected, perhaps subconsciously, was one worth catching, and she could use Vaiking for bait. If she thought any more at all about Joel, it was a fleeting acknowledgment that he had been quite satisfactory, but of course no one to concentrate on for a career and, besides, the adventure with him was over. Now here was his officer, and this was something else, something new, and, fortunately, much, much higher in rank. Vaiking could launch her on this new conquest, but that would about take care of him. And, unaware that he was being so used, Joel did just that.

He and the Captain, with Lafe Tucker, were drinking the inevitable coffee near the fire, after the wagons had drawn up for a nooning just east of the crossing on Alder Creek when Kim, dressed in her finest, demurely made her play. No gun-fighter could have prepared more carefully or conducted the affair with greater efficiency.

"I would love some of that good-smelling coffee, Mr. Tucker," she begged sweetly, moving into the circle of conversation. "Oh, hello, Joel! Is this your officer?"

With no escape, Vaiking nodded.

"It is," he said shortly. "Captain Ravalier. Captain, sir, this is Miss Kim Raggensworth. She is the daughter of Governor Raggensworth of New Mexico." He concluded lamely, "She is goin' east to school, I hear."

Kim laughed gently. She kept her eyes on the Captain, caressing him with them, knowing, expert that she was, that she aroused and deepened his interest in her as she did so. Men are so easy, she thought happily.

"That is what *they* think," she said archly, to Vaiking's explanation. "But I didn't promise to *stay* back there, not for a little minute! If I don't like it I'll be right back out here on the plains with some other train going west. Don't you think I should if I truly don't like it, Captain, sir?"

What was he to say? He agreed this would be a wise move for her, adding some customary nonsense about the country being glorified by such women, and she, in her turn, piling it on with a compliment, first about the way he sat his horse (the most direct course to a Cavalryman's heart, she knew instinctively, was to praise his horsemanship), and then, becoming more warmly personal, admiring the twin sweeps of his brown mustache. By then Ravalier was hooked, Vaiking abandoned and knowing it, and Kim well on the way toward a fresh conquest which, Tucker sardonically noted, at least would not disrupt his everlastin' train further.

The wagons that evening drew up a mile north of the fort, circling just south of the Trail, and almost immediately Ravalier and Kim rode off toward the post, walking their horses through the warm evening, side by side, chatting like old friends and totally unconcerned about the rest of the world. Vaiking, aware that he had lost out, feeling anew the flush of helplessness before tumultuous events, and sure of his inadequacy to meet them, sat glumly on a wagon tongue. Tucker mended a piece of harness nearby, and Dipsy Jack worked his cud.

"That's the way with some wimmen," said Jack helpfully, sympathizing with the Corporal in his torment. "They ain't constant, most of 'em."

Silence greeted his remark, and he took that as an invitation to go on.

"One thing you got to say fer Injun wimmen, they is generally constant." He spat a brown stream at the fire. "Some ways they ain't as jobbin' as white wimmen. That is to say, they ain't jawin' at you all th' time, an' demandin' an' refusin' an' havin' a goddam mind of their own. But they is constant, generally speakin', eff'n you don't leave 'em fer too long at a spell."

"No doubt," said Lafe, neatly sewing the leather straps into place. "I ain't had no experience of 'em myself. You, soldier?"

"No," conceded Vaiking. "I never chased women much,

and not Indian women at all. Didn't speak the language and never felt I understood 'em well enough."

"Pity," said Jack philosophically. "Man gits attached to one woman alone, especially be she white, an' it puts him at a disadvantage. He gits to figgerin' he *owes* her somethin'. First thing you know he builds a house, an' plows a field an' then he ain't worth a hoot in hell forever more."

"I often seen it happen that way," agreed Tucker cheerfully.

"But they is one good thing, about wimmen," continued Jack. "It ain't no trick at all to fergit 'em." Vaiking glanced dubiously at him, and Jack explained, "Git you another one. Thet is a sure cure fer broodin' about th' one that got away."

"That ain't a cure," said the Corporal morosely. "That gets to be a habit."

Ravalier brought Kim back to the train before dawn and Tucker pointed it east again at sunup. Three days later it reached the rolling hills along the Pawnee River above its junction with the Arkansas, and Vaiking, with deep relief, turned it over to a detachment from Fort Larned. He and his detail left that same afternoon, without a backward glance, riding swiftly westward toward Fort Chopps. Joel hoped, somewhat wistfully, that he had gotten Kim pregnant. He hoped someone had; it would serve her right! He didn't know it was impossible.

IX

Vaiking's detail clattered into Chips and made for the corrals, while the Corporal sought out the Captain to report in. He found him in the orderly room, handed over the mail and dispatches he had brought, and reportedly briefly. Neither mentioned Kim Raggensworth; it was as though they had met her separately in some other, more distant, existence. Vaiking rode his tired horse over to the Quartermaster corral. He unsaddled, rubbed the animal's sweaty back down thoroughly with gunny sacks, tied him to a feed rack and stole a good measure of corn for him from the QM supplies, then forked hay to him. In common with most old soldiers, Joel took meticulous care of his horse, especially this one, the rangy bay. When he had the authority he saw to it that his men cared well for their animals, too. "Out here," he was sometimes heard to say, "a man travels on four legs, not two, or he don't move at all." He tried to make sure that, when there was a mission to be performed, he had four sound and willing legs to carry him on it and bring him back.

The Corporal stopped by the mess hall for a cup of coffee and chunk of stale bread, all the supper he or his detachment would have this night, and then walked the length of the parade ground to the first barracks, which he shared with

about half of the company. Smoky lamps dimly lit the
interior. Some of the men were huddled around a couple of
crap shooters at the near end. Others lay on their bunks
thinking of decent food, or women perhaps, or whiskey or
home. Vaiking took his blankets past them to his own bunk.
He made it up before he noticed that Riley's bed, next to
his, was stripped down to the rawhide cross-hatching of the
frame itself.

"Where at's Riley?" he asked Swanson, lying on his
back on the next bunk. Swanson hesitated. "Riley's dead,"
he said, then, adding, "You ask that son of a bitch Sergeant
where Riley's at. He knows."

"What'd he die of? How come he's dead, Swanson?"
cried Vaiking, looming over the soldier, who stared at the
low ceiling and didn't appear to notice.

"He died of a overdose of Nero. That's what he died of,"
he repeated.

Swanson had spoken softly, but his voice penetrated.
Other men clustered about the two, all those in the barracks
except the crap shooters at the other end and two or three
watching them. Their sharp cries, or an occasional gam-
bler's moan, seemed unnaturally loud in the thick fog of the
room, but the others paid no attention. Morris explained:

"Nero claimed he lost a pair of goddam socks, or
somethin', an' come through here like a cyclone," he
volunteered. "He said he found 'em on th' floor next to
Riley's bed, but Riley said he didn't know nothin' about no
socks. Nero knocked him down, an' Riley let his Irish
temper take over an' slugged Nero in the belly. Nero got
madder then, and when Riley still wouldn't admit nothin'
took him over to th' orderly room. That's all I seen."

"What happened there, Harrison?" growled Vaiking.
The clerk bit his lip.

"The Sergeant told the Captain this man was a thief, but
wouldn't admit it. The Captain asked Riley questions, but
Riley didn't answer, or didn't answer right. Nero said they'd
been other thefts lately, an' he suspected Riley did 'em, so

th' Captain says, 'OK, Sergeant, work th' truth out of him some way,' an' Nero took him to th' hay sheds back o' the blacksmith shop, an' I don't know nothing after that."

"I sure as hell do!" muttered Swanson. "Me an' Gunderson was on guard. Nero had us string Riley up by the thumbs like he usually does to some poor bastard about oncet a week. When Riley still wouldn't talk, he built a load of rocks onto his back an' kept pilin' it higher an' heavier so as to pull down harder an' Riley yelled till you could hear him a mile away I'm surprised you didn't hear him clear to Larned! Finally, God help me if it didn't pull out Riley's thumb by th' goddam socket. It popped like a cork when it come out! If I hadn't seen it, an' heard it, I wouldn't never have believed it."

The faces of the men looked ghostly gray in the hazy light of the flickering lamps. "What happened then, Swanson?" prodded Vaiking bleakly.

"Riley was bleedin' like a stuck hog. He still didn't say nothin' an' looked like he never even heard Nero. He didn't look at nothin', nor seem to see nothin'. Then that bastard ordered him strung up again, by his right thumb an' left wrist this time. We had to do it, him standin' over us an' mad as hell an' all. So we done it, but Riley was bleedin' bad.

"Then Nero stripped the load off'n Riley's back. To me he seemed insane, and I think he was, sort of. He was so goddam mad! He took out that welted blacksnake an' whipped him unconscious, if he wasn't already unconscious, like I think he was. Finally he says, 'Cut him down, goddam him. We can't get nothin' outta him when he don't keep conscious!' an' we cut him down, an' he just curled up there on th' floor of th' hay shed, an' never moved an' never said nothin' no more. He died there."

Irrelevantly Vaiking wondered, "Who did steal them socks?"

"No one knows," said Gunderson. "Like as not no one

did. Nero just blew up outta his own damn black heart for
no reason except he's Nero, is what I think."

Joel Vaiking wordlessly threaded his way to the door and
shouldered through it, making his way to the cooling sweep
of the Arkansas, gleaming wetly in the star-studded night.
He sat on its bank, almost oblivious to the stinging
mosquitoes, stared at the dark, turgid waters, and tried to
sort out his tumbling emotions and clouded thoughts. He
had liked Riley, damn it, but Riley was dead, and now he
wasn't the main thing, good a man and cheerful as he had
been. The big thing was how come a man like Nero had the
power to murder another man, and get others to help him,
when most of the men either sympathized with Riley or
were not sold on him being a thief. It wasn't right. No man
should have that power. Yet the Army was the Army and
authority was strictly defined, and you had to have authority
or you would have no Army, and without an Army pretty
soon you would have no country, or no country fit to live in,
anyway. How was a man to look at this complete wrong
wrapped up in a general good?

Blindly, savagely trying to make sense of this vast
enigma which had concerned other men for ages past,
Vaiking at last groped to his feet and, almost without
realizing it, found himself with Kate, in bed with her,
talking out his concerns and puzzles with this woman who
always listened and when she talked, spoke sense.

This time she was silent for so long he thought maybe she
hadn't heard.

"You live in a man's world, Joel," she said, then, at last.
"I'm a woman. I can't see things like you do, quite. I see
them as a woman does, in bits and pieces, in details. Maybe
you should do that a little, too, if you can."

"What do you mean, Kate?"

"It just seems to me you can't deal with whole armies and
such. Not even with this whole Army, all the time. What

you must deal with is separate situations, and with men, individual men."

"Like me and Nero?"

"Kind of like that, Joel. What I'm sayin' is that you got to figure out in your own mind what a man should aim at in a certain situation, and how he should think and work at it, an' when you get that all straightened out, maybe you can see then how an Army should work, an' how soldiers in an Army should conduct themselves. Then maybe you can see what's right and what's wrong and where you fit in. Maybe."

Vaiking was silent for a long time.

"You got any whiskey, Kate?" he asked suddenly. "I think we need a jolt or two."

X

Colonel Henry Tangle exhaled noisily, slouched lower in his hard-backed wooden chair, and idly watched through the open window a growing dust whorl spinning across the parade ground of Fort Brackett, near the juncture of the Solomon and Smoky Hill Rivers. Dust was like the Cheyennes, he growled to himself. Those Indians were scorching half of the central plains by now, and if they weren't whipped onto a reservation somewhere the contagion would no doubt spread through the Northern Cheyennes and Sioux above the Platte and the five bands of Comanches below the Arkansas. Like a plague, this Indian business was. Once you had an outbreak you had to move fast to deal with it, or at least isolate it, or pretty soon it swept out of control like a monstrous prairie fire no man or no units Congress appropriated for could rightly handle until it burned itself out. Any reasonable man would say the Army's job was impossible. Congress wouldn't appropriate enough money for sufficient men, or even to equip and arm them satisfactorily, then expected the troops to do the job anyway, and raised hell when the Army failed even through no fault of its own.

He sighed again, deeply, and combed his heavy beard with his strong fingers. This was one of his moody, introspective days. He was aware of it, and in a few minutes he would fight it, and go out and inspect the pack mules or cavalry horses or something and improve his attitude. But right now he was damn good and moody, and not ready to rouse himself.

Funny thing about the Southern Cheyennes going out, just when it seemed they would come in. You couldn't always tell why an Indian acted like an Indian, of course, but there might well have been some special reason for this outbreak. It burst about the time Kavalier had that fight, coming in from his long scout. Yet a fight wouldn't necessarily send the Indians out, as he well knew. It would more likely bring them in, if it were successful. Indians well understood such blows, and responded to them, generally speaking. He knew that from his many years' campaigning against them, against the Yakimas in the northwest, and the Pit Indians, and the Modocs and the Apaches. There was no officer in the Army who better understood the Indians than Colonel Henry Tangle, although he never admitted it, even to himself. His job was to pacify whatever Indians he was up against at a given time. Pacification was more important than fighting them; you fought them only to pacify them. But you fought them hard, when you did it.

Secretly Henry Tangle admired the Indians, and sympathized with them, and understood their violent nature and reaction against the incomprehensible, onrushing whites, even though they were as many as the blades of grass and obviously, even to an Indian, unbeatable in the long run. Personally he wished there might be a place set apart where the Indian could roam wild and free and hunt buffalo and make his light-hearted war as he always had, but he knew that it was impossible. Nothing could stop the white men coming in, even though many whites were little improvement over the Indians. But it was inevitable. He couldn't stop them, and wouldn't if he could, probably, but he would do what was possible to see the Indians got a fair shake when they finally did come in, though no warlike people ever settled onto a reservation, he well knew, until they had been soundly whipped. That was his number-one job: whipping them. His number-two job was getting them resigned to reservation life, disagreeable as a reservation would be to many of them.

Henry Tangle frowned once more. Damn peculiar, the Cheyennes going out.

That was why he had called for a noncommissioned officer and a detail from Fort Arnold Chopps to come up here and escort him to that post. He didn't need an escort, and if he did he could take one from Brackett, easy as not. But he wanted a responsible enlisted man to whom he could chat en route, and from whom, without his becoming aware of it, extract information no officer would ever reveal about Chopps and its activities of late. Tangle was a sly one, his subordinate officers sometimes said, though well beyond his hearing. He had ways of eliciting information without anyone knowing his true purpose, and sorting it and filing it in his massive head until it had become a storehouse of facts, all kinds of facts, that made him the most knowledgeable and best-oriented officer in the Army, at least among those concerned with Indian affairs. He talked with almost everyone. Not only with military personnel, but with scouts, Indians, emigrants, miners, border riffraff and all the others. The only people he ever talked with were the women, the wives, the emigrant females, the whores. Henry Tangle had no aversion for women. He was married himself, with a contented wife back east, but he felt he might somehow be taking unfair advantage of women's proclivity toward gossip, and he wouldn't want to do that. Frankly, he was uneasy with women, didn't rightly understand them, unless they were squaws, and while courteous to a high degree with the ladies, he was uncomfortable amid their sort of aimless chitchat and gossip.

And now he had Josiah Pickerfield to worry about, on top of a raging Indian war.

Pickerfield was—well, you had to see him and hear him

talk to believe it. Tangle smiled grimly as he thought of him, in a sort of fatherly way, for Pickerfield was a charge, and if the Colonel didn't wet-nurse him he would be killed before they even reached Chopps. Probably fall out of a buggy and break his neck, if the Indians didn't get him first.

Josiah Pickerfield was a Quaker, and looked it. He had an upright fringe of white hair fencing a bald spot that at least assured that he would never be scalped. His blue eyes were lively, never at ease, flickering from one thing to another, jostly as a bird's. His nose was large, his face clean-shaven, his back a bit stooped, his arms and legs almost grotesquely thin, and his manner inquisitive, stubborn and not exactly unintelligent, Tangle would admit, but determined to the point of blindness. Very determined.

Pickerfield was going out to make peace with the wild plains Cheyennes, which, Henry Tangle speculated gloomily, would be about the best joke those Indians had ever heard from the white men.

The Quaker thought all he had to do was let loose a smoke signal or something and call the tribesmen in, talk reasonably with them, discover their grievances which, of course, they must have, settle them, find a nice roomy place where they could plow and raise vegetables, give them plenty of blankets and bright clothes, send their children to school somewhere, and the Indians would become playful, friendly, willing and peaceful wards of the nation forevermore. Tangle snorted. Good God! And he had to call off or suspend a war while this fool tried to impose his Quaker notions on the most turbulent of frontiers. He didn't even want the Army's help! Christ!

Yet he had to admit that Josiah Pickerfield was not completely an ass. He was a man you could talk to. He was just ignorant as hell about Indians and especially wild ones. But orders were orders, and if Washington wanted to give Pickerfield a try, and directed Colonel Henry Tangle to render him "every assistance," he would meticulously do just that—for a couple of weeks, anyway, and then get on with the war. He repeated to himself what he knew well, you had to whip Indians before you could talk with them. There was no other way. He was forced to agree, however, that Pickerfield's notions of justice and fair play for the tribesmen were very similar to his own. But you simply had to outfight them before you could bring those factors to use.

The orderly knocked, came in, and clicked to attention.

"Detail arrived from Fort Chips—er, Chopps—sir," he said. "Corporal with it. Name is Vaiking. Does the Colonel wish to see him now?"

Corporal, hmph, thought Tangle. He'd asked for a "responsible" man, and thought he'd get at least a Sergeant. Maybe this one would do, though.

"Send him in. I'll see him now," he told the orderly, and leaned back in his chair again and waited.

Vaiking saluted stiffly.

"Corporal Vaiking reporting to the Colonel as ordered," he said crisply.

Tangle indicated a vacant chair.

"At ease, Vaiking," he said informally. He was a very informal officer, for all of his efficiency. "Have a seat. Pleasant trip?"

"Nothing unusual, sir. Six days. Six men came with me. All the horses are sound and ready to return whenever the Colonel desires. One needs a shoe tightened."

"Better have it taken care of right away. Where are they now?"

"At the Quartermaster corral, sir. The detail is rubbing them down. The shoe is being tightened at the shop."

Tangle was pleased. This big noncom knew his business. He cared for his horses and cared for his men, in that order. So did the Colonel.

"Tell me, Vaiking, is that Indian, Big Ass, still at the post?" The Corporal nodded, and the officer said, almost as an aside, "I'd like to talk with him. I suppose there is someone there who can interpret?"

"Yes, sir. Guide, name of Dipsy Jack."

"I know him," said the Colonel shortly.

He glanced out the window again. Another dust whorl was making up. He looked sharply at the soldier.

"Exactly how was he taken, Corporal?" The report had told the story in round terms, but with no details. Tangle always desired details.

"The Indian come to the flat across the river from the post, with his woman, an' seemed ready to talk," said Vaiking. "Captain Ravalier, Jack, an'—an' a noncom went out to talk. Big Ass threw down with his lance at the Captain, an' he was knocked in the head an' brought to the post more or less out." He added, "He was brought in about a jump ahead of a lot of Cheyennes who busted out of the hills beyond to interrupt the talk."

"Did Jack crack down on the Indian and capture him?" wondered the officer.

Vaiking hesitated, almost imperceptibly.

"No, sir," he said.

"Who did?"

"The noncom, sir."

"Who was he? Report didn't say."

Again Vaiking hesitated. Perhaps he reddened a little. But he was honest.

"I was, sir."

Henry Tangle was satisfied. A shrewd judge of men, red or white, he now knew considerably more about Vaiking than the Corporal had revealed in words. His bearing had demonstrated him to be a veteran soldier. His uniform sleeves revealed traces of the larger patches of a past higher grade. Tangle had discovered that he was honest, that he was intelligent and could act decisively. That was enough for him. He could depend on information he might extract from Joel Vaiking.

XI

The party, including the Colonel, his aide, his striker plus Mr. Pickerfield and the escort, started with the dawn for Chopps, on the long freight road toward the distant post on the Arkansas. The trip would be lengthened by the fact that Pickerfield chose to ride in an ambulance. But this could prove an ultimate blessing, Tangle conceded, since to put the aged Quaker on a Cavalry horse for that long a ride might precipitate a catastrophe. He was content.

Traveling until about 3 o'clock each day, the group usually made camp along some watercourse. Colonel Tangle enjoyed the open life, but he was a meticulous camper. He secretly approved of Vaiking's efficiency in setting up and taking apart their bivouacs. On the third day they began to see buffalo, and for that night stopped on the banks of Walnut Creek, some distance above old Fort Zarah. Tangle did not wish to endure military formalities and niceties when he did not have to do so, and avoided the more heavily traveled trail to the south, where he might meet small Army parties as well as business caravans or even emigrants, though there were not likely to be many of the latter at this time of year.

The Colonel demanded the utmost in obedience and respect from his subordinates, but he was no martinet. He was, in fact, a most unmilitary man who judged others not by station but by character.

This evening, supper over, he settled himself by the crackling elm fire, sipping his coffee and tugging at his beard. He invited Vaiking to join him, as Mr. Pickerfield and his aide already had done.

They talked of this and that, back and forth, and Vaiking felt himself warmed toward this commanding, interesting figure who dominated the fireside conversation and the men surrounding him as he dominated whomever he met. At times like these, he spoke to others more as equals than as an officer of considerable rank conversing with men of lower station.

Tangle took a deep draught of coffee and exhaled his pleasure. He glanced at the luminous sky, broken out in a rash of stars. The moon had not yet risen, and wouldn't for two or three hours. The prairie was still save for the long and deep, rising howl of a distant wolf, touching off a cacophony of coyote yips and barks. The air barely stirred. A horse stamped away a mosquito as it drowsed on the picket line. The guards, beyond the glow of the firelight, were silently alert.

"This is the part of Army life I like," commented Tangle to no one in particular.

"Why, for goodness sake?" demanded Pickerfield in astonishment. "There's no one here. It's, it's a—a—wilderness, that's what it is. Heavens, man, I can see some day this being settled with tidy farms and schoolchildren and herdsmen coming in from the cow barns with pails of milk and happy families around a table eagerly devouring steaming suppers. Then this will be a heavenly place. But it assuredly is not that now!"

Tangle peered at him from the depths of his gray eyes, a faint smile tugging at his mouth beneath the beard.

"Well, now, Mr. Pickerfield," he said mildly, "that might be 'heavenly' for some men, but it's not for others. I can do without all those smiling families. I would rather have a lousy buffalo an' a red Indian chasing him to hell and gone, an' a wolf to eat what's left after the squaws are finished an' to howl about his full belly afterward. Then I like to lay me down with a rising prairie wind drifting through my beard an' watch the stars, an' not know whether I'll wake up tomorrow or have it end tonight with a prowler's knife through my gizzard. That's what I appreciate—freedom, and demands, and a little loneliness thrown in, too. But mostly the freedom. True freedom."

Mr. Pickerfield twisted his fingers together tensely.

"There's no such thing as 'freedom,' really," he objected earnestly. "You say you're 'free,' and perhaps you feel so, but you are an officer—what about your enlisted men? Are they free? How can you truly be free if the enlisted men under you, all the thousands of them, are not free? Could you be free and not be an officer? Could you be 'free' if you were not in the Army, say? I tell you, sir, it is not possible, in the way you describe. The only true 'freedom' comes with a sense of doing what is right for those around you in line with God's will. There is no other freedom."

Tangle thought about what the Quaker had said. One thing, could an enlisted man feel the freedom he himself felt? He wondered.

"How about that, Vaiking?" he asked abruptly. "Do you feel 'free,' or do you feel enslaved, being a soldier. How long you been a soldier?"

"Since first Bull Run, sir," replied Vaiking. He considered the Colonel's other question. "I don't know, sir," he went on thoughtfully. "A soldier's got to follow orders. When they come greased, sort of—that is, direct an' trim, like all normal orders an' all—it's easy, an' you have a sort of freedom within the framework, you might say. Other times, though, it's different, I think."

"Other times, like what?" asked the Colonel easily.

Vaiking shrugged his shoulders slightly.

"Sir, I don't rightly know," he admitted. "When orders comes down that you're used to, or that you expect, rather, you can follow them out an' it doesn't do nothing to your freedom. It's what has to be done an' every man has a part he's got to play. That's all right. But sometimes a man gets an order he can't—just can't—follow. What he's to do then I don't know. I don't rightly know. It's hell, sir, gettin' an order like that an' knowin' you are supposed to obey it, an' goddam it, sir, just not bein' able to. Maybe that's when 'freedom' comes into it all, sir.''

"Exactly," chortled Pickerfield, rocking back on his seat, with his thin arms clasped around his knees and his blue eyes crinkling. "Precisely! This is when your 'freedom' is meaningless, Colonel Tangle. For you, as an officer, it is perhaps more possible to know it than for Mr. Vaiking, as a soldier, but in either case there comes a time when it cannot be 'freedom,' but must be 'obedience.' It depends upon whom your obedience is to. Mine is to God and to man. That is true 'freedom' for me!"

Vaiking surprised them by bursting in with a question, from where he did not know.

"You mean for you there ain't no 'authority'?" he demanded. "What does that do for keepin' things goin', like we got to?"

Josiah Pickerfield fixed him with an unblinking stare.

"Young man," he said, not being a bit pompous, "you have asked a very, very important question. Yes, sir, I do believe in authority—God's authority. And I ain't bein' other-worldly when I speak so, as the Colonel here no doubt believes I am. I mean God's authority as directed to you through your conscience. You have a conscience, you know. It might be heavily encased, you being a soldier for so long, an' during your—what you might call—formative years, but it's there, like it is in all men. Yes, you must obey authority. Man's authority, even. As you say, it's to 'keep things goin.' We all have to do that! But supreme to you, an' to all men, is your conscience. That is the highest authority of all, because that is God speaking to you. When you run against a conflict between man's authority and

God's authority, you can obey one or t'other. That's what we mean by free choice. But if you obey man's authority when it conflicts with God's authority, you're takin' a step toward darkness an' when you obey God's authority when it conflicts with man's authority, you step toward light. No matter what happens to you because you do it. That's what I mean, son."

Vaiking considered what the lively old Quaker had said.

"Maybe what you tell me is true," he commented reflectively. "But I am a soldier. I got to obey, if I am to be a soldier. What if what you call God's authority won't let me obey what as a soldier I must obey? What happens to me? What happens to the Army? What happens to everything?"

Again Pickerfield stared at him before replying.

"God's authority, son," he said, "works not only through men; it also works through men's agencies, even armies. Agencies, and armies, have consciences like you do. Like I do. When orders come down out of consciences, then you can feel no conflict, if you understand perfectly. It is when orders come not through Army conscience that you can feel conflict, an' that most likely is God conflictin' with a improper Army order, is what it is. Then, no matter what 'happens' to you, you are in the right. That is because the only integrity a man knows, that means anything to him, is his own. It produces clashes, all right—as when an Indian's basic integrity conflicts with a white man's conception of right as opposed to wrong. But that results, after the fightin', in progress, I do believe."

The fire snapped hungrily at another stick of elm wood.

"All I got to say," said the Colonel, neither believing nor disbelieving the argument, and not following all of it, if the truth be known, "is that that is a hell of a way to run an Army. You'd have every man bein' his own officer, his own commander. We couldn't man a single post anywhere with that kind of reasonin', and keep it manned."

"Not at all, Colonel," objected Mr. Pickerfield, rising to his feet. "You would have every man obeying every order the best way, out of the depths of himself, out of his personal convictions, with no coercion, obeyin' because the orders were just, an' he knows it, an' obeying because he feels in his bones that he must always obey just orders. Then, Colonel, you would have true freedom, not for officers such as you, alone, but for all men."

Josiah Pickerfield took himself off through the darkness toward his bedroll, beyond ear-shot of the campfire. Henry Tangle heaved a sigh of relief, got out his stubby, blackened pipe, filled it, tamped the moist tobacco firmly into its charred bowl, and lighted it with an ember.

"I learned as a young officer out on the coast that the Army is not God Almighty, and shouldn't be the whole life of anyone, not even its officers and men," he said between puffs, talking either to himself or for the benefit of this big Corporal who sought so eagerly to straighten out his own complicated thinking. "The Army is a tool. Only a tool to get the job done. So is every other human organization, just a tool. That means that none of them are ends in themselves. Man is the only such in the world, and that goes for white man and red alike."

"Then why are we fighting them, sir?" asked Vaiking, his brow wrinkled in puzzled concentration.

"Because you've got to be pragmatic. That is, take things as they actually are, and work from there. The fact is that, right or wrong, this is Indian country but it's going to be white country soon, and the red man, if he is to survive, is going to have to be fitted somehow into the white culture, even if he don't slip in easy and without pain. The Army's job is to fit him in. My aim is to do it as smoothly as it can be done, and as painlessly, too, for the benefit of both white man and Indian. But it's a tough row to hoe. Neither side offers much help to a man, or understanding, either."

He drew a few times on his pipe.

"But the Army is just a tool to get it done. A man who serves in it must submit to the workings of that tool, because otherwise it would be ineffective. But he must remain a man, too. If he's going to do that, he must accept responsibility for himself and for what he does, and how he reacts to orders an' such. Thus, normally, he would obey the orders that come down to him, but when in his judgment the orders would have to be disobeyed, for example, to accomplish the mission which the Army is in business to do, then he has to take that responsibility on himself, and if he is punished for it—as happens, occasionally—he must take the punishment, too."

Joel Vaiking felt as though a great light had dawned over him, as the import of the Colonel's words, added to what the Quaker had said, soaked into his mind.

"Other times," the Colonel went on, "a man might get orders that he knows are wrong for some other reason, and if he knows this well enough, and feels strongly enough about it, he must, to retain his manhood, refuse to carry them out, too, and take the punishment for his refusal. That has always been my course and I must say I've been set back, or punished, as much as any officer of my rank in the Army. And I know I'll be punished some more, from time to time."

He poked at the fire with a stick.

"But I'm still a soldier, an' I still believe in the Army, an' I'll never be corrected for doing anything in the Army but trying, as I understand it, to make it do better what it is supposed to get done."

Tangle turned then to the subject uppermost in his mind.

"Tell me, Vaiking, about Ravalier's fight on the Cimarron," he said bluntly.

Unaware of the Colonel's underlying purpose, the soldier related as briefly as he could the story of the sharp engagement, up to the time the Cheyennes had scattered and fled upstream.

"That all that happened?" demanded Tangle.

"Yes, sir," replied Vaiking. "That's all of the fight, sir.

We never seen no more of the Cheyennes then until Big Ass showed up on the Arkansas. Heard about 'em, though."

The Colonel puffed thoughtfully until he got his pipe going well again.

"You sure that's all, Corporal?" he persisted. "What happened, maybe, after the fight? No more Indians?"

Vaiking hedged, twisted uncomfortably, stared into the glowing fire.

"That's about all, sir," he said. "We left next morning to come back."

"'About' all, Vaiking? What do you mean, 'about' all? What else occurred?"

The noncom knew he was trapped. He felt the sweat prickles under his blouse.

"I don't know's I recall anythin' else important, sir," he stalled.

"Important or not important, let's have it," growled Tangle shortly.

"There may have been one or two prisoners picked up, is all," he mumbled lamely.

"Prisoners? Ravalier's report said nothing about prisoners. What became of them? Were they men or women, maybe? Tell me about the prisoners, Corporal."

"They was only one, I know of."

"Answer my question, goddam it, Corporal!"

"Yes, sir. There was only one, I know of. I didn't see what happened to her."

"Woman, eh? How come you didn't see what happened to her, Corporal? You was First Sergeant then, weren't you?" That was a shot in the dark, but a bull's eye. "*What happened to her*, Corporal? Who was she?"

"Dipsy Jack told me she was Dust Devil's woman," said Vaiking softly. "Next mornin' when I left she was goin' upstream toward where her people'd run."

"Next morning! What happened to her that night? What the hell became of her in the morning? You tell me true, Corporal, or you'll rot in the guardhouse forevermore!"

"Yes, sir," said Vaiking miserably. He did not fear the threat, which he realized was more or less perfunctory, but he was now ordered to do something that violated his long soldier's training, to reveal a sordid tale that he believed had best be left buried. Nevertheless, he outlined the story, because he was a soldier and he was ordered to relate it, and somehow he felt that revealing it was in line with the Army's true mission, as the Colonel had just explained must be the goal of a soldier or an officer.

When he finished, Colonel Tangle puffed savagely at his pipe.

"Corporal," he said at last, knocking the glowing coals from its hot bowl, "I don't like to drag such a story from a soldier who can't help himself. It's not my nature. But I *had* to find out what you told me, why we got this Indian war on our hands, an' you told me why. I thank you for it. For your information," he added, rising to his feet, "Ravalier will never be told where I got the information or even, for that matter, that I got it. It's a matter over an' done with and can never be undone. Now we got to wind up this war some way, but there'll be a lot more good men lost doing it, on both sides.

"The Captain is a fine combat officer and he will be a key man in concluding it, I have no doubt of that." Turning away, the Colonel stalked off into the night, muttering to himself, "If he was just as good a man as he is a fighter, he'd be President, or something."

XII

When Bony Nero read off the assignments the morning after the Tangle escort concluded its mission, to no one's surprise, least of all to Vaiking's, the Corporal found himself named to stable duty again, along with four privates. The bleak fury of Nero's reaction when the Captain named Vaiking to go to Fort Brackett had not been lost. If there had been a worse chore than stable duty, the Corporal knew Nero would have sentenced him to that instead. Envy works in blunt, predictable ways, even when it is not justifiable, and Joel could sense that the tension between him and the First Sergeant, fueled by Nero's imagined slights, would soon head up.

Vaiking still had mentioned nothing to the First Sergeant about Riley's murder, and perhaps he never would. You couldn't fight the Army or the system and stay a soldier long. Nor did you cry, if you were an old soldier, even for others. It was sort of an existentialist way of life; that is, you took things pretty much as they were, day by day, knowing you couldn't do a thing about yesterday, but hoping today came out all right. You kept your mouth shut as long as you could. If you were smart, and had survived for long, you generally kept it shut for good. Riley's death, however, as described to Vaiking, had been sheer murder, no doubt of that, and he resented it still.

Ravalier let Nero run the company about as he chose, as he had permitted Vaiking to run it before the Cimarron. Vaiking, however, had run it differently. Now Nero, jealous of the greater regard held for his predecessor by most of the men, was increasingly vindictive, spoiling for a fight, and determined to establish his own preeminence in the only way he could—by brute strength.

This might be the day.

It was 3 o'clock before Nero got around to the corrals to check up on his stable detail. He had obviously been planning his visit and stewing about it all day. He was in a black mood. He stepped slowly down the picket line, and back along it behind the tail-switching horses. He stopped behind Ravalier's mount. Vaiking and the privates continued hammering away, fixing loose boards in the feed rack. They were aware of the Sergeant's progress, but pretended not to be.

"Vaiking!" Nero bellowed so sharply that the horses nearest him raised their heads, ears back, awaiting a blow. "Vaiking, why the hell ain't the Captain's horse groomed yet? Here it's almost recall already."

The Corporal straightened up, hammer in hand.

"He's been groomed," he said evenly. "Rub your damn' sleeve over him and see if he ain't."

"I say he ain't been touched with a brush all day," insisted Nero bleakly. "Who done it, like you say, you?"

"No. Woody groomed him first thing."

Nero's eyes surveyed the group, straightened up now and watching the interchange with true soldierly eagerness. This might be good.

"If that yard bird 'groomed' him, he must of done it with a sagebrush; he didn't go over him with no groomin' brush. You get you a brush yourself an' come here and work him down while I see it's done right."

Nero balanced himself forward on his toes like a fighter,

flinging his words like individual challenges he expected to be taken up. Vaiking shrugged, dropped the hammer and picked up a grooming brush. He stepped over to the Captain's chestnut and, starting at the neck, groomed him expertly, thoroughly, cleaning each hoof as he came to it and finally combing out the black mane and tail, making the animal gleam in the late afternoon sunlight. Nero watched intently, but said nothing until Vaiking had finished.

"That was for Woody's not doin' it right first time," he said then, as the Corporal turned to put the brush back on its hook. "Now do it again, fer your not makin' Woody do it right first time."

Vaiking stared evenly at the First Sergeant. He threw the brush at Nero's feet. He, too, seemed to rock forward on his toes.

"Brush him down yourself, if that ain't good enough, Nero," he said in a low tone, the words coming out flat and separately. Nero flicked his glance over the listening detail, switched it back to Vaiking.

"A order is a order, Corporal," he said. "You groom that goddam horse or face the Captain refusin' to do it!"

Joel gazed up and down Nero's huge bulk, placed his hands on his hips.

"Captain got to fight your fights for you, Nero?" he demanded. "You been spoilin' fer a damn big one ever since the Cimarron. Now's as good a time as you'll ever get." He didn't really suppose Nero would take the dispute to Ravalier, but you never could be sure. Nero's eyes widened, then narrowed. He almost grinned.

"Let's go into th' other corral," he suggested. "It's more private."

Vaiking followed him through the gate into the smaller, adobe enclosure. The walls were seven feet tall, too high to be looked over. The gate was of poles, though. The four privates lined the other side of it, arms on the upper poles, excitedly peering over them at the two antagonists, as they peeled off their shirts. They were about of a size, Nero perhaps an inch shorter, but beefier. They each had fists like sledges, and their muscles were stone-hard from the rugged plains life. They were ready for this one.

When they squared off and came together it was like two buffalo bulls colliding. Neither knew or cared anything about defense; each was out to cut the other down frontier-style, which meant any way possible. Vaiking doubled on Nero's face while the Sergeant kicked the other in the groin, and when he writhed in pain, hammered the back of his head, belting Vaiking into the dust, then diving on top of him, the two of them rolling over and over, half slugging, half wrestling, reaching for each other's eyes, nose, mouth and throat, twisting and turning over and over and over. But when they broke and came up gasping to start all over again, it was Vaiking who arose first, who stepped in and with all his strength smashed his fist deep into Nero's belly, causing him, in turn, to double, gasping for air. This time Vaiking straightened him with an uppercut to his jaw, then knocked him head over heels with a flurry of crushing rights and lefts. Nero lay dazed, rolled, got to his hands and knees and stayed there, head down, dripping blood, shaking his great skull to clear it.

"Get up, you son of a bitch," growled Vaiking between gasps, "or I'll kick your guts out! That was for me. Now get Riley's licks!"

The taunt stabbed deep, and Nero came to his feet with a roar. His charge, head-first like a giant bull, caught Vaiking in the midsection and again they rolled and twisted on the dusty ground, raising puffs of pulverized earth as they thumped each other, and again it was the Corporal who rose first and caught the Sergeant with a ripping jab that laid him flat on his back. When he struggled once more to his feet, unwilling or unable to surrender, all but defenseless, Vaiking surged in and with left and right fists, battered him into the wall where his head thudded against its unresisting surface, and he sagged downward, eyes glazed, to lie unconscious at its base.

Only then did the four soldiers peering over the gate utter a sound.

"Whyn't you kill 'im when you had the chancet?" demanded Woody, with a broad, approving grin. Vaiking struggled into his shirt, wiping the dust and sweat from his unmarked face, and the four clustered after him like a brood of chicks as he made for the barracks. Behind them lay Nero on his back in the corral dust, dazedly attempting to focus his eyes on a white cloud overhead and remember clearly what had happened.

Colonel Tangle and Captain Ravalier conferred in the latter's office, with Special Indian Commissioner Josiah Pickerfield silently teetering his chair back and forth against the wall, across the room.

"My instructions from General Sherman are that we extend every assistance to Mr. Pickerfield," rumbled the Colonel. "I gather that he is to make one supreme effort to call in the Cheyennes, and I shall of course fulfill my orders in every way possible. If he should fail within a reasonable period, say two or three weeks, I intend to proceed along more military lines to settle the whole business. That will mean making Fort Chopps the center for a campaign aimed at seeking out and smashing Dust Devil's village, beating his warriors in an open fight, if they can be brought to it, and hurting him so badly that he will be forced to bring his people in or see them destroyed. It will be one or the other."

Ravalier nodded thoughtfully.

"Is it the Colonel's intent to assemble his striking force out of the 12th Cavalry, or some other regiment, perhaps?"

"The 12th, I have decided, will be the backbone for it. A couple of companies of the 17th Infantry and maybe a battery of artillery would comprise it," replied Tangle. "Officers concerned have already been put on the alert, with a view to accomplishing the concentration swiftly, should it be necessary. It can be done within a very limited time, once ordered."

"I trust and believe that it will not be necessary," interjected Josiah Pickerfield. "If we can establish contact with the Indians, I am confident we can bring them in for a talk. If we can do that, peace will inevitably follow."

"I agree that you can maybe get a peace if you can bring them in," replied Tangle. "Especially with winter coming on. They wouldn't mind being fed and fattened during the winter for more deviltry in the spring. Problem is, how."

"I believe we can do it, establish contact, by the use of that Indian held prisoner here, Big—ah—Rump, or whatever he is called," said the Quaker delicately.

"Let's talk to him," said Tangle quickly. "Call Jack and have them bring in the Indian." Ravalier issued the instructions.

Big Ass showed few traces of his confinement, except that his eyes seemed a bit duller than usual, his manner less arrogant and animated. But he was still self-possessed, still contemptuous of his captors, still hostile.

"Explain to him I am the representative of the big soldier chief, and Mr. Pickerfield here is a representative of the big white chief at Washington," instructed Tangle. "We have come to talk with him about this war."

Dipsy Jack and Big Ass exchanged gutturals.

"He say he 'representative' of big Indian chief, to sort of square this council off," commented Jack dryly. Tangle grinned involuntarily, then recovered. "He say he is a big war leader, not a chief, though. I already knowed that, but he sayin' it so we won't try to make a deal with him."

"I believe we can come to some understanding if we can define the misunderstanding that exists," said Pickerfield. "Ask him why his people went to war, what they want, what they object to about the whites, what it will take to make peace?"

"I don't think we need to go into all that—just how can we get his people in for a talk," interrupted Ravalier.

"Let him answer the Commissioner," said Tangle bluntly. The Captain subsided.

A staccato interchange followed. Jack, the only man present who understood Cheyenne, also clearly comprehended the situation. He had served Ravalier for a long time, and knew how the land lay, as he would have said. He was well aware what had set the plains afire, because he had helped bring it about, and he was not now ready to reveal the details nor to bring on Ravalier's head the axe which might glance from the officer's skull to his own. Ravalier's deadly secret was safe with Jack, as the officer fervently hoped.

"He say," said Jack, after a long conversation, "that Dust Devil went out mostly to save the buffalo range, he's afeered th' white man goin' to take over."

Tangle fixed him with an unblinking stare.

"Jack, you tell the damned truth or I'll nail your hide to the wall!"

"So help me God thet's exactly what he done said, Gin'l," protested the scout. "Let me ask him agin, though."

Another lengthy exchange followed, and the scout turned back to the senior officer. He knew Tangle didn't believe him, but he also knew Tangle had no other source of information. He felt reasonably safe.

"He say it's the buffalo range, Gin'l," repeated Jack blandly.

Pickerfield took over then, explaining through Jack all the benefits peace would bring the Indians, that continued war would be a disaster for them, that the whites were as many as the grasshoppers and that it was inevitable they would surge in increasing swarms across the plains, that the buffalo were doomed, that the Indian would have to learn a new way of life and that the generous white man would feed him abundantly while he learned, or forever if he chose not to learn. How much of this Jack translated to Big Ass was problematical, but he did explain that Pickerfield desired him to take a message to Dust Devil, inviting him, urging him even, to come in and talk under a truce, and to bring his important men. To this Big Ass agreed gruffly. He consented to invite Dust Devil in, but not to assure that he would come in.

"And tell him if he don't come in, the soldiers will run him down and give him such a clearing out he'll wish he had," growled the Colonel.

There was not even the pretense of sincerity when Big Ass shook hands all around at the conclusion of the parley. Ravalier ordered the Indian's spotted pony brought around, and his lance and shield recovered from soldiers who had seized them as authentic souvenirs of life on the plains, and they, too, were handed to the Indian. He vaulted upon his pony and swung silently down toward the river. He waded the animal through the swirling stream, gaining the open, grassy bench beyond. He turned then to face the fort, a defiant figure on a wild, free horse.

Big Ass seemed to straighten on his pony. He raised his lance over his head and stabbed with it toward the fort and screamed a war cry that could be heard across the river, vibrating among the squalid buildings—fierce, angry, cruel, implacable. The Indian whirled his pony, dug in his heels and sent it scampering toward the bluffs beyond.

"I hope he returns soon," said Mr. Pickerfield optimistically.

"It's my guess he won't return at all," muttered Henry Tangle. "That's the last we'll see of Big Ass until we see him dead or defeated in battle. That's what I think."

Ravalier and Jack were silent.

XIII

First Sergeant Bony Nero never said a word to Vaiking after their fight, except in line of duty, and that was the way Joel wanted it. Nero was too much of a soldier to cry about his beating, but too much of a man to forget it. He was perfectly correct in all his relations with the Corporal, but Vaiking knew he would wait until he died to catch his enemy in an error or overstepping himself.

Yet this was no cause for concern. Vaiking had always been careful not to push beyond his grade. He had no fear of Nero and he could sense that no one else knew about their fight except as it seeped from the lips of the four soldiers who had witnessed it and circulated in the lower echelons of the troop.

The soldiers at Fort Chips knew the details of Pickerfield's purpose, of the interview with Big Ass, and of the Indian's mission almost as soon as the officers themselves did, for such was the way of the soldier and the channels of communication at the frontier forts. Joel Vaiking was one of the first to be made aware of the Quaker's mission, of course, having heard of it at Brackett before the party reached the Arkansas. He hoped Pickerfield's mission would succeed, but had a soldier's distrust for anyone's ability to talk out difficulties before some heads were broken.

But he found the Commissioner always genial, always ready to pass a word or the time of day during the long period of waiting for the Big Ass mission to produce something. Despite himself, he felt drawn toward the Quaker. He found his beliefs, and his positive approach to a nebulous frontier intriguing, even if sometimes perplexing and, in the long run, he firmly believed, utterly futile.

"What if the Cheyennes don't come in?" he asked, one day.

"I am confident they will," assured Mr. Pickerfield. But he was a man of candor as well as integrity. "However, should they not, the matter would be out of my hands, even though not beyond my conscience. All men have a responsibility for what happens to all other men."

"You mean you have a 'responsibility' for what happens to them Indians, even if they don't do what you think is best, and are beyond reach?"

"Exactly. Because they may behave in error does not mean that they are beyond my concern, nor does it lessen their own value as human beings, wherever they are to be found."

"What about all those whites they slaughter an' mutilate an' maybe even torture?" challenged Vaiking. "Ain't they your concern, too? Or is it just the Indians you are concerned about?"

Josiah Pickerfield smiled, then replied thoughtfully.

"You have a way of asking significant questions, Mr. Vaiking," he said. "I admit it seems as though my concern is wholly for the Indians, that it is not at all for their white victims. That, however, is not the case. Were the circumstances reversed, my concern—my paramount concern—would be for the whites. It is equally for them, in any case. My purpose is basically peace first, then justice for each individual, then prosperity an' development for all. That is what my range of purposes call for. The key to peace right now is the Cheyenne people, an' the basic element to bring peace is justice to the Indians, I think. Once we have peace we can take up the other things, one by one. But we cannot consider them until we have peace."

"How can you have peace until the Indians is whipped, the way the Colonel wants to do?"

"It is one thing to settle the war by blows, militarily, but then you have on one side a victorious people, an' on the other the vanquished, and it is very difficult to create justice in such a situation," said the Quaker with deep earnestness. "First you must have the essentials of peace, which is right thinking, in every man. Only then can true peace, true justice, true progress come about."

"How do you get man to think 'right,' Mr. Pickerfield?"

"You start with yourself. You have already asked the basic questions, and I have told you what I think about it. You must not seek to conquer, but to see justly within yourself toward other people. To do that requires a start, a beginning, and then a period of germination and of development, which in your case I judge is already far advanced. It must work itself out by itself, but if the first impetus is correct, it will."

"You know something, Mr. Pickerfield? I think th' Colonel is really a lot like you. He sees Indians like he sees whites. There is no value difference for him between whites and Indians. He sees only men, good and bad. But just men."

The Special Commissioner pondered that proposition, then replied slowly: "I think you may be partially right, Mr. Vaiking. But he sees all men as men—alike on the level of war and enforced discipline and enforced peace. On a level of combat, you might say. On the other hand, I see men alike on a basis of justice and love and goodwill and peace-through-consent. I feel there is a difference. I naturally think my level is the higher, though I respect Colonel Tangle's views."

Pickerfield mused over the thought a bit. When he spoke

again, he looked straight at Vaiking, until the Corporal felt that the Quaker was speaking directly at some hidden element of his mind, struggling for identification.

"You see, Mr. Vaiking, war leads to war," said the white-haired old man. "Excess leads to excess. Someone abuses an Indian, and he feels compelled to avenge himself. When he does, another white man seeks to punish him for it, and the Indian again retaliates. Somebody has to stop this evil chain of events, break the ring. One man—one man alone, perhaps—could do it. But he must, or it is not broken, and injustice somewhere in the distant past, inciting retaliation and vengeance over and over again, has brought us to today's impasse. One man, who has the vision, can break it up, if he should find himself in a key spot. But he has got to do it. He *must*."

Despite the high hopes of the Quaker commissioner, the Cheyennes did not come in.

Day followed day as the dust spirals chased one another across the burning autumn landscape, but no Indians appeared across the river or in any other place, desiring talk, wishing to settle their bitter war with the white interlopers. Each day's delay reinforced Tangle's conviction that the only means of bringing them in would be to beat them in. Yet day followed day, and the plains seemed as empty as the surface of the moon, but the soldiers at Fort Chips knew that out there still lurked the savage, whirling hordes intent upon the obliteration of every wagon outfit, isolated ranch, hunting party and small body of troops within their striking power. The war continued in sporadic, vicious violence.

At the end of two weeks Colonel Tangle issued orders that set into motion the vast complex operation that had been prepared in his previous instructions to garrisons of half the frontier military posts in Kansas and Nebraska. Columns of troops, some abbreviated and others of good length, began to assemble at Chips, bringing a new bustle, fresh life, as they filled the establishment to its planned capacity, and overflowed up and down the tree-lined river.

Added to K Company, already there, M soon joined from the Republican, the only 12th Cavalry unit based farther west than K. From the east and north came B, D, E and G companies, with supply units and pack outfits. Companies B and M of the 17th Infantry also swung in, to camp up the river, beyond the horse companies; and Battery D of the 24th Pack Artillery arrived with its fat, well-trained mules and quiet efficiency. The sutler's store was transformed overnight into a major meeting place, and Chips came alive with men, munitions, horses, mules, wagons and supply units. The ring of the several blacksmiths' hammers sounded day and night; the noises horses and mules make were magnified; and Chips, formerly confined to a dozen or so adobe buildings, sprawled now over two miles or more of Kansas plains.

For Corporal Vaiking the growing bustle and confusion were welcome. He found relief from his own strained thoughts in the single-minded preparations which engaged all personnel at Fort Chips, those stationed there regularly and the new arrivals alike. Even Nero seemed almost pleasant, or at least more nearly tolerable, as he directed the men with purpose these days, instead of the make-work pointlessness of routine garrison days. The soldiers reflected the enthusiasm. Even Tennessee turned his bitter grudge against the First Sergeant and Ravalier toward the enemy, if briefly, and Woody, developing under Vaiking's guidance into a pretty fair soldier, was a barrel of energy.

Vaiking communicated something of this new life to Kate, who, he thought, should be making a killing at her profession, what with all the troops in. But for some reason she had taken to rejecting almost all advances, although she always held the door wide for Vaiking. He visited her often, as a matter of course, as much because he enjoyed talking with her as because he needed her for an outlet to his energies.

There were daily drills, marches and countermarches, horse- and man-training programs, and even a little target practice, although an economy-minded Congress frowned on that. A couple of newspaper correspondents from the east wandered in and appeared to write daily dispatches, although how they sent them out was a mystery, and none of their papers ever reached Chips, at least until the giant expedition got underway.

Filtering in among the soldiers and officers were the scouts.

Most were full-bearded men, silent usually, tobacco-chewing or smoking, dressed in bizarre costumes, men half white and half Indian for the most part. Many of them had lived with the Cheyennes or other plains tribes and had absorbed ideas of dress and novel customs from them. There were half a dozen painted Indians, too, of the Pawnee or some other tribe farther east, hired by one company commander in the event expert trackers were needed. No one expected them to fight.

During all this time scouts were sent out in parties of two or three, in all directions, to locate trails, work out those most promising, and to bring back information when they had any. These reported to their company commanders who, if they judged the information valuable, passed it along to Colonel Tangle. From his office at Ravalier's headquarters, he assembled information and planned the operation. On a huge wall map, parts of which were plainly labeled "unknown," although the scouts were familiar with all the terrain represented, he plotted the routes of the several guides and the information returned by them.

Dipsy Jack and a scout called Gridey returned late one day after a week's circuit to the south, and reported directly to the Colonel that they at last had stumbled onto what he most avidly sought. They had located a congress of trails which they judged to be those of a large band of Cheyennes, not too old, leading southeast from a point four days to the south. They believed that the enemy was moving camp from somewhere to the west toward the Canadian, or Washita, or the North Fork of the Red, or some stream even farther south, although they wouldn't go too far because that was Comanche country.

"How many lodges would you guess?" asked Tangle thoughtfully.

"Couldn't rightly tell, Gin'l, but they was a lot of 'em," said Jack. "Gridey thought they was eight hundred, an' I figgered they was more, but how many I couldn't say. But they is Cheyennes, we is sure o' that. If they is any more Cheyennes out, they ain't in this part o' th' country."

The Colonel tugged at his beard, then turned to Ravalier.

"Officers' call in two hours, here," he directed. "All commanders to be present, an' any other officers not needed for duty."

He picked up a pencil, and turned back to the map.

When his officers had assembled, he surveyed the group calculatingly, pleased by what he saw. All but one or two were veterans of the Civil War, and looked it—tanned, composed, competent, ready for any sort of task along the lines of their profession, most of them heavily mustached, as befit cavalrymen with pride in their branch of the service. As fine a lot of officers as any commander could ask, Tangle thought proudly.

"Some of you have been growling for action," he addressed them. "Now I think you can have it." He smiled inwardly as he noted the delighted grins on the faces of the younger officers. "A couple of scouts, Jack, here, and Gridey, have found a trail they think means the Cheyennes are moving their main camp south of us, maybe to the Canadian or the Washita for the winter. With any luck we can surprise them there, an' maybe settle this war with one blow."

He shoved his ruler toward the pertinent points on the map, the position of Fort Chopps, the route of the

Cheyennes as reported, their probable goal, and the way he intended to follow southward in pursuit of them.

"We will have to keep well back, letting the scouts establish and maintain contact," he said, "until they go into camp, which no doubt will be in the timber along one of those streams. Once they are busy establishing themselves they will be fair game, and I trust we'll hit them hard. A good, resounding blow can end this war with one campaign, an' no matter how some of you gentlemen enjoy late autumn or early winter campaigns, I will settle for just this one." His officers laughed politely, as much because of their regard for Tangle as at his gentle sally. He had few enemies among his junior officers; all the officers he chose to battle with were his seniors.

"This is Wednesday," he said slowly. "We will leave camp at sunup, Sunday. Company K will lead out, first day, and the order of march will be given you later. All ailing men and animals will be left here unless they obviously will become fit for duty shortly. Questions?"

Like a well-greased wagon, the vast preparations moved forward smoothly and quickly, each officer, his competence honed in long years of campaign and battle, preparing his own small segment of the whole until it was poised, aimed and ready to move out. The moment had come. And then disaster struck.

Late on Friday, Colonel Henry Tangle suffered one of those uncommon, but not unknown, accidents coincident to life on the plains. Cantering his horse back from B Company's bivouac downstream, his mount thrust a foreleg into a badger hole and fell, throwing the officer in a jolting mishap that broke his left leg between knee and hip, and he was taken to the post hospital, in great pain and thoroughly incapacitated. He immediately insisted, however, on an emergency officers' call around his bed, even before the cast was set.

"Gentlemen," he interrupted their sympathetic remarks, "it is the fortunes of war, the ill-luck we never think about and do not anticipate. But that is neither here nor there." He grimaced with a twinge of almost unbearable agony, then resumed. "The campaign, of course, must go on. Plans are too far advanced to be reversed. I have decided in this emergency to turn over temporary field command to Captain Ravalier, a brevet Lieutenant Colonel, as his post has been most heavily involved thus far, and his combat record is proven and good —as are the records of all of you, tor that matter. Ravalier will assume his brevet rank for its duration, and you will report to him for orders. He is aware of my intentions, as are you all, and I will confer with him further before you leave. You must go now, so the doctor can look after this damned leg. Good luck to all of you! May you find the enemy, attack him, and have a good success!"

Vaiking spent most of the last night with Kate, enjoying her body and frankly discussing the coming campaign. Not once did he mention any predictable future for the two of them, nor did she. Right now was enough for her, and it was all she felt she had any right to enjoy. A brutal life had nearly convinced her that the course of existence was inevitably downward, and there was no point in anticipating the worse things to come. But right now she was happy, happier than she could ever remember herself to have been.

"Take care, Joel," she cautioned, as he kissed her good-bye before dawn. "Take care."

"Sure, Kate," he promised. "We may not even get in a fight, an' we'll sure run into nothing we can't handle, with all this force."

Shortly after sunup Sunday, amid choking clouds of yellow dust and with the blaring of a post band rocketing among the structures around the beaten parade ground, K Company led out, crossed the river by the rock-bottomed ford, followed by the other units in order, with guidons listlessly twitching, grained horses on this first day eagerly stepping out, pack mules and wagons in slight disarray, but in their proper positions, and the artillery, bringing up the rear, out of dust range from the freight guards, and acting as sort of watch for the tail end of the long column. The company positions would be rotated, day by day, so no trooper had to eat dust more than another, and so each would serve as forward and as rear guard in turn. It was a professional column, one of high efficiency, and Colonel Tangle, wheeled out of the hospital, his bed overlooking the scene, felt a thrill of pride, and of envy, too, as he watched it cheerily grind out of Fort Arnold Chopps.

"Good luck!" he called to Ravalier, who had reported to him before the departure. "And for God's sake, Ravalier, remember an Army ain't one man, even one good man, with a good company behind him. Hit 'em to end the war, not to build a reputation, an' bring back every last soul if you can!"

Ravalier swept back his mustaches from either side of his mouth. His one brown and one blue eye glittered in anticipation, the Colonel too far from him to see the slight tic over the one. He saluted sharply as he spun his horse.

"I'll remember, sir," he promised. "We'll not come back without a fight, if we can find 'em—and I'm right confident we can do that!" He cantered away to the head of the column, square-shouldered, riding easily, the picture of a Cavalry officer off to war.

Far to the south, that same bright morning, Dust Devil and Big Ass, finished with three days of making war medicine, led their horde of painted, half-naked savages out of the great assembly toward the northeast, the cavalcade bright with paint and nodding plumes. They were eager now for a fresh raid against the frontier, the last of the year, while the people established themselves in winter camp among the thick cottonwoods along the quietly flowing stream. It was low, at the end of the dry season, and would remain low during the long winter soon to come, but it would flow some water until spring. It always had done that.

The lodges were filled with dried buffalo meat from the fall hunt. The women were busy tanning hundreds of hides for winter work of repairing tepees and making war clothing and other garments. The old men were holding forth, day by day, with their feasting and recollections, and boasting of long-past exploits, grown more heroic with repeated telling. Children played in and out of the streams, using their small bows and arrows as their fathers used the mighty ones in hunt and war. Pony herds grazed, in thousands of animals, on both banks of the main stream and far out on the plains, storing up what fat they could for the lean winter months ahead when cottonwood twigs and snow-covered buffalo grass would be all they could forage until spring.

It was a busy scene, but an ancient one, that the warriors left as they filed out at dawn for the northeast and this one last savage raid before the deep snows came. When it was over the fighting men would come home to the warmth of their lodges, to their wives and the people, loaded with scalps and loot, they hoped, to rest and feast and await spring and fresh, green grass once more.

And on that same day, red-haired Kim Raggensworth disembarked at Westport from a St. Louis river-steamer, to the vast relief of the captain and the consternation of the male passenger list, which she left in something of a shambles. Oblivious to such disorder, she primly made her way with several young men in tow, a willing escort, to a Miss Agatha Quill's boarding house, arranged for a comfortable room, and informally dispatched her current admirers to discover what trains might be making up for a late season push for Santa Fe. There wouldn't be many, but there ought to be one or two.

"I found the school they sent me to utterly incredible," she explained to the wise Miss Quill, who knew when to hold her tongue. "Impossible! I am simply dying to get back to my dear father at Santa Fe, and shall do so at the *very* earliest opportunity. Don't you think that is wise, Miss Quill?"

"If it is what you desire," said the older woman noncommittally. "I am sure you know best whether it is wise."

XIV

The dusted blue column of many units, gradually coalescing into a compact whole, worked south, day by day. Most often it marched with two companies abreast, in order to shorten its length and make it more manageable in the unlikely event it should be attacked or run across hostiles. Cavalry and Infantry companies made up the twin columns, with the wagons and pack outfits in the center for greater protection. They met no Indians on the march, however.

Ravalier held an officers' call each evening, and every morning he sent the scouts and the Pawnees forward to range a mile or five miles ahead of the command, searching for sign, seeking the enemy, as only such plains-wise human ferrets could do. The march generally was southerly, but a bit to the west, making for the broad trail Jack had discovered, intending to follow it down to the winter camp, wherever that might be, hoping by a cautious advance on the aging trail to catch the enemy unawares and smash him before he could rally.

"We should be cutting the trail tomorrow or next day," Ravalier told his officers on the fourth evening. "I want each company tightened up, with no straggling, and most of all, no hunting buffalo to either side, in front or behind—

107

no hunting, anywhere, under any circumstances. Understood?"

The officers nodded. Stirring up a herd might precipitate a chain reaction among other bands until lurking Indians, in hunting parties or otherwise, would learn that there were intruders in the vicinity.

"All the scouting from now on will be done under my orders only," the officer continued. "Don't send out your own scouts or the Pawnees any more. Keep them in hand, near the column. We must avoid at any cost the Cheyennes' learning of our approach."

Again the officers nodded silently.

"If there are no questions, that is all."

Ravalier called Dipsy Jack over.

"The way I figure from your report, we should be cutting that trail tomorrow perhaps, Jack. What do you think?"

"That's about the way I calc'late, Gin'l," agreed Dipsy, chewing his tobacco thoughtfully. "She was headin' toward the Canadian, which we is, too, an' I believe we ain't too far off."

"I want you to go ahead before we move out, which will be at 5 a.m.," said the officer. "Scout southward as fast and as far as you can, an' try to cut it, then work along it more slowly. Be very cautious, Jack—I don't want those Indians to suspect we're in the country. Take a soldier with you, and Gridey, too, if you want. When you strike the trail, send the soldier back to tell me where it is, and its course, and we'll cut across the angle to save time."

"We'll do 'er, Gin'l," promised Jack. "Better give me Vaiking. He's a good man in a pinch, should it come."

Vaiking rode south with the two scouts, leaving the bivouac about 4, long before sunup. Jack rode his spotted Indian pony, and Gridey a mule, Vaiking his long-traveling, rangy bay, a mount he swore could run a week if necessary. The horse had a hammer-head, giving it an ugly first appearance, which probably was why no officer had snapped him up somewhere along the line. But he had all the bottom in the world, and Vaiking had acquired him through an intricate series of swaps and machinations, the detailed nature of which was known only to old Army noncoms. He felt, and justly, that the horse had more endurance than any other in the company, and maybe in the regiment.

They headed straight out, but avoided riding the crests of the swells, remaining deep in the troughs, so they would not be skylined for hostile eyes to observe. There was a sharp tang in the air, presaging some imminent winter howler perhaps, but the prairie gleamed as the sun arose, its colors ranging from the dust-gray of the buffalo grass through the washed blue of the occasional sage to a sort of yellow where the sunlight glinted. To the west a tight scattering of buffalo darkly speckled a distant ridge, grazing so peacefully it was obvious they had not been run by hunters recently. A band of seven antelope whirled and danced along before them. They, too, were an assurance that no Indians were about. One great condor floated in the sky far overhead.

"Sure wisht I was where that ol' bastard sails," commented Jack, a bit wistfully. "If I was I could see plumb into Texas, an' everythin' that moves or doesn't move. We'd ought to make scouts outta them damn birds!"

"Too many already is callin' us buzzards," objected Gridey, whose few comments usually were to the point. "Was such birds made scouts it would give 'em cause to think we all *is* actually buzzards."

Vaiking laughed.

"Maybe eagles would be better, eh, Jack?"

"Okay, eagles. Not buzzards," agreed the scout amiably. "But it's still a hell of a good place to see from, where they usually is at."

A few moments later Gridey's mule spun aside at the warning of a rattlesnake. The scout easily stayed with his animal during the abrupt maneuver, gazed nonchalantly back at the coiled snake, and rode on.

"Wonder what'd be like to be bitten by one o' them?" he murmured.

"Hit ain't so bad," said Jack. "I was bit oncet, up north o' the Platte. Big one. Must of been six, seven feet. Nailed me in the left leg. Only thing was I didn't have no whiskey, which is a sure cure if you kin hold enough of it."

"What'd you do, with nothing to drink, Jack?" questioned Vaiking.

"Wal, I was stuck for a while, tryin' to think what I should do," recollected the scout. "Me with no whiskey. All I had was my last chew of tobacco, an' finally I stuck that on an' tied it tight. But it was touch an' go."

"Whether you lived or died?"

"Hell, no. Whether I used th' chew that way or swallowed it fer a anteedote. I thought o' that, but figgered I might not be able to keep 'er down, so I stuck it on th' outside instead. Hated to do it, though, it bein' my last chew."

"Did it work?" asked the Corporal.

"Reckon so," Jack responded, his busy eyes sweeping the skyline ahead and all around. "Leastwise here I am."

They struck the trail in midafternoon, a broad scarring of the earth's surface, marking the passage of many people and hundreds, or maybe thousands, of ponies. Scratches of dragging lodgepoles marked the course as plainly as wind-bent grass, but the trail also was heavily trampled out by hoofs, dog tracks, the moccasined prints of women and children. There was no litter along the way. Nothing ever was discarded in a Cheyenne camp or on the trail. Everything, no matter how useless to its present owner, would find a purpose with someone else. The people were like a cyclone funnel, sucking up the earth's substance as they passed over and carrying everything along.

The general bearing was southeast, as Jack had reported, toward the timbered river bottoms of the south plains, where good wintering grounds were abundant. There the buffalo still congregated, assuring that should dried meat

give out, fresh could be found not too far distant. Deer and
elk, too, browsed among the cottonwoods of most of the
bottoms, but the people disdained such when buffalo was to
be had. Elk, or even deer, made, as some of the scouts
asserted, "mighty poor doin's," but it was food in an
emergency.

Where the white man had come, however, the game soon
disappeared, whether before the muzzles of his guns or
because it could not live in close proximity with him no one
knew and many argued about. The people could live on the
inhospitable plains forever, allowing for times of famine
occasionally, though in relative abundance most of the
while, but a single white man was a disruptive force, a
white family served always as the focal point of change, and
a white settlement reversed the whole process of nature. It
was basically this that the Indians fought against, if so
futilely, even when they could not spell their reasons out.

For an hour more the trio rode warily along the trail,
keeping to the troughs constantly, and crossing an occasional ridge only after minute examination of the way
ahead, even though the trail itself was now several weeks
old. They passed one great camping ground, covering a
mile or more, the scouts pointing out for Vaiking the worn
circles of the many tepees, the ashes of the campfires, the
bones of the buffalo, gnawed clean first by Indians, then by
their ever-hungry dogs, and finally by the wolves and
coyotes of the prairies. The people were moving slowly,
Jack indicated to the Corporal, while Gridey poked around.
Ten, twelve miles in a day was good traveling for them, for
there was no hurry. The seasons came and went, and there
was time for all life and social events, even if there was a
blazing war going on in distant places against the white
interlopers, carried on along the emigrant trails and spear-
heads of settlement by boiling bands of warriors, a long way
from their base camps.

Down here, far to the south, there was no war, or so they
thought, and the people's lives went on pretty much as they

had for thousands of years. There was time enough. Soon they would arrive at a place the chiefs had selected for the winter. The fighting men would return one day. The snows would come. The people would feast, and visit, and stage their absorbing ceremonials, and make love, and boast of past deeds, and guard their horses, and wait until spring had opened up the plains again. Such was life for the Cheyennes in this season, as in all seasons past, as far as the memories of even the old ones went.

"Seems not to be such a bad life," mused Joel to Dipsy Jack.

"Bad life? It's a hell of a good life, I'd say, especially if you got a little woman or two in a snug tepee keepin' the fire goin' an' enough woolly robes around to keep th' chill out."

"Makes you wonder why it's got to be destroyed for another way of life."

"Some wonders an' some don't," said Jack blithely. "Me, I don' wonder none atall about it. I lives with th' Cheyennes awhile, an' then I scouts fer th' Army awhile. So long's I get somethin' to eat, an' a little whiskey an' tobacco, it don't make me no difference what comes to pass."

"But what will you do when the Indians are gone, and the Army with them, an' there's no room to live like you been doing?"

Jack squinted at the late afternoon sun, scanned the skyline before replying.

"Them things is goin' to come about, sure as we're ridin' here," he agreed. "But this life'll last no doubt as long as I do, an' arter I'm gone I don't give a damn what happens. A man jus' does what he can as long as he can, an' takes each day one at a time, is all."

"Seems to me you have to worry just a little about the consequences of what you do," said Vaiking, more to himself than to Jack. "A man ain't all by himself, all alone." Although he didn't realize it, Pickerfield, the Quaker, was speaking through him.

"That ain't the way I figger it," countered Jack decisively. "What I do is fer myself alone, to get me through that knothole ahead, an' oncet on t'other side, I got no mind to look back, or, fer that matter, to even one side or other. Jus' get through the knotholes. That's me."

Gridey and Jack drew up at the base of a slope where the trail topped a swell in its meandering course toward the Canadian.

"You'd best go back to the Gin'l an' tell him where we is at," advised Jack. "Tell him we is on the trail, follerin' it about as fast as he is comin' on, an' that we'll go ahead along it until we find somethin', be it several days. Tell him to pick it up an' come right along, an' we'll let him know plenty of time afore he strikes th' camp. But tell him this ain't to say they ain't war parties out still, millin' aroun' somewheres, an' to keep his eyes open an' the Pawnees as a close-in screen, so's he won't be surprised by any one of 'em."

Vaiking nodded. He took the back trail, cutting to the right as Jack had indicated. He smelled the chip fires long before he saw the massive Army encampment along a creek bed to the northwest, and found Ravalier up, just finished with officers' call, and impatiently awaiting word from his scouts.

The Corporal reported Jack's advice, which his officer took seriously.

It was then that Ravalier told him he was named acting company Sergeant, and curtly dismissed him.

Vaiking cared meticulously for his horse, ate bacon and a little bread and drank a cup or two of coffee, and finally bedded down. It had been a long day. So now he was Sergeant once again, to work more directly than ever under Nero. From First Sergeant, to buck private, back to Corporal and now to Sergeant once more. It was not unprecedented in the postwar Army for a man to whip up and down through grades so swiftly, but it was no common thing either.

He reflected on the day when he had lost his grade, not through any failure, but his stubborn mental block, which he still had, although now, after productive conversations with the Colonel and the Special Commissioner, he could understand it a little better. Maybe he could explain it away in his mind. But he hadn't lost it, and in an Army job it would provoke crises still to come, as he was thoroughly aware. Yet he knew no life but the Army. He couldn't conceive of any other, now. When a man came at odds with the demands of his profession, what became of him?

Vaiking did not know. But he went to sleep wondering about it.

XV

In the dim predawn light the encampment stirred like a prehistoric beast rousing itself. The stock was fed, brushed down and after a bit of bacon and hot coffee the camp was swiftly struck. Once in the saddle, the command moved steadily out in the form laid down by Ravalier at officers' call last night. Well in front, as always, roved the point and a slender screen of scouts, whose task it was to root out and trip any ambuscades that might have been laid during the dark hours.

Other detachments screened the flanks of the column, a quarter of a mile to a mile out on the plains on either side, and there was a final small unit warily bringing up the rear, far enough back to be out of the dust, collecting stragglers and alert against a surprise swipe at the command's tail by some free-roving war band. It was the movement of a single command, though vastly larger and more complex than one company alone, but the unity was there.

It was totally self-contained. When it had passed on there was nothing behind, no strings to any fixed base or fort, no lines of communication, nothing. Nor was it drawn toward any such beyond the horizon ahead. It was a floating island of war-seeking men and supplies, free to move in any direction, with no other concern but its mission. Unless it succeeded in locating its enemy, and in attacking him, it would be a failure, and Ravalier was determined that it would not fail.

Vaiking rode with him, guiding him toward the broad hostile trail the scouts had located and presumably followed still, somewhere to the southeast. Neither the Corporal nor the officer talked much. Each was wrapped in his own thoughts.

The Corporal fervently hoped the campaign would result in a sharp, clean fight, so there would be no problems, nothing to regret, no inner conflicts to resolve, of the sort that had accosted him in recent months. He was not averse to battle, any more than the Indians were. Man against man was one thing, and not at all evil, Vaiking believed. It was the side issues that bothered him, and led him into strange ponderings about the whole frontier endeavor, the conquest of the plains from the natives.

He recalled the glint he had seen in the eyes of Big Ass when that damned redskin, captured, was held for Ravalier's decision in headquarters, the wild, free, unafraid, even contemptuous glare upon the white enemies surrounding him. Vaiking had seen comparable expressions on the faces of an occasional white under similar circumstances. Always it had aroused his secret admiration. When it appeared on a white face, it invariably brought a certain respect on the part of the captors, whoever they might be. But there was no such admiration on the part of the whites when they dealt with a captured Indian who exhibited identical courage and defiance.

Why?

For that matter, why basically was one race fighting the other? In order to seize something the other had, like these worthless plains? Buffalo country, and little more. Likely it would never amount to anything more. That couldn't be it, entirely.

Because of Indian hostility toward the whites? What about white hostility toward the Indian? Which came first;

which began it all? How had this warfare begun, why did it continue, how would it end? Who was in the right, anyway? Or was anyone all right or all wrong?

Vaiking didn't know the answers to such questions, but he felt their weight, nonetheless. Hell of a way for a soldier to begin to think. A soldier, as Ravalier sometimes said, wasn't supposed to think, just follow orders. When action was called for, he was to fight, but between-times just a body to be ordered about, and to move about, and not to think of it at all. Here he was puzzling over the very nature of a soldier and the job he was supposed to be doing. He didn't know where it would all lead, but he couldn't see any good coming from it.

The great column, moving more slowly than the three scouts had the day before, struck the Indian trail about an hour before sundown, and turned into it, as Vaiking directed. He asked whether he should now drop back to K Company, with the command's way quite clear ahead, but Ravalier indicated he desired him to remain with him, and he did so. Still neither spoke much. The officer called a halt just short of the Indians' former camping ground, directing his officers to make the bivouac as tight as possible. It was created with dispatch, according to the familiar pattern.

At officers' call the commander outlined his present plans.

"They depend upon events," he said. "But our purpose now is to follow this trail as fast as we can, while taking precautions against surprise or jumping the enemy before we're ready for him. Jack thinks they'll be camped along the Canadian or the Washita or some similar stream, somewhere southeast, where there's timber enough for a winter camp. We depend upon him, what he finds. He is scouting ahead, but will let us know when he finds where the Indians are located. We will assess the situation, and try to deliver our blow as hard and as much of a surprise as we can, and hope to finish this war with it alone."

Vaiking found the field duties of a company Sergeant

better in one way than those of a Corporal, and not so good
in another. He had more of the supervision and direction
that he liked to do, especially since the Captain was
otherwise occupied. But he came more directly under Nero,
which was all right as long as both attended strictly to their
jobs, but there was an ominous undercurrent warning
Vaiking that Nero was his enemy still, and would be as long
as they were in the same company.

Yet the First Sergeant seemed eager to help make the
expedition count for something, as though he had an interest
in it beyond his grade. It was the mark of a good soldier,
and in some ways Nero was such. The heightened prospect
of action diverted his attention from his feud. He was busy.
His mind was occupied. He was not concerned, for now,
about crossing swords with Joel Vaiking once more.

"You tend to your company, an' I'll take care of my
business," he once told his antagonist.

"That's what I aim to do, Nero," was the quiet reply, and
that is the way it had been, most of the time, since leaving
Chips.

Four full days the command lumbered along the main
trail of the unwary Indians, camping the last night on the
bank of an unnamed creek, which emptied into the
Canadian River. A light snow, the first of the autumn, sifted
into camp, melting as it came, at least at first. Here, shortly
after the men had gone to sleep, Jack slipped in and awoke
Ravalier.

"Jesus Christ, Gin'l," he complained. "Them guards o'
yours is useless! I come right in betwixt 'em, horse an' all,
an' never disturbed a one of 'em nor even inspired one to
sneeze! Why, Dust Devil an' his Cheyennes could slit the
throat of every man in the command afore anyone was
awoke!"

The officer grunted.

"They smell worse than you do," he said. "That would
probably alert the guards, if nothin' else did. What you got
to report, Jack?"

The bearded scout bit off a big chew of plug tobacco before replying. He spat once.

"The Cheyenne is camped on th' Washita, Gin'l," he said. "I don' know how big their camp is, fer I just seen the upper end of it. But from the smoke I could tell she's a big 'un. It goes on down th' river a ways, an' maybe includes more Injuns than just those whose trail we been a-follerin'. But I don't think the bucks is with 'em, at least some of 'em ain't. Their hosses is gone, although they is plenty left around the camp, an' from what we could see they ain't too many fightin' men thar, at least not in th' upper camp."

The officer considered the report in silence.

"Gridey still down there?" he asked.

Jack nodded. "Tol' 'im to wait an' find out what he could," he replied.

"Tell me how the land lays."

"We kin get within a mile o' the camp, er half a mile, if we is lucky, especially if we do it arter dark. They is a rise we kin come over which'll put us right in the middle o' th' upper camp, which I think we kin take without too much trouble, especially since th' men ain't thar, most of 'em. If we kin do that, mebbe we kin roll up th' camps downstream a ways. But you can't tell fer sure."

Again Ravalier was silent, reflecting.

"How far we got to go?" he demanded.

"If you was t'other Gin'l, I'd say three days; bein's it's you, though, I'd figger two days of damn hard goin', to put us behind the ridge. Thet would include a night march, er most o' th' last night, anyways, so's we could hit 'em come dawn."

The officer blew on his fingers to warm them, folded his arms, with his hands underneath.

"Christ it's cold," he grumbled. "Better get some sleep, Jack. We'll start before dawn. This damn' snow won't make our approach any easier, unless it quits."

"Wal, yes an' no," responded Dipsy Jack. "It'll hold down th' dust, an' unless them Indians is huntin' their back trail, which ain't likely since they knowed they already pushed the game aside when they moved down toward the winter camp, they won't be aroun' to spot us. I'd say th' snow is a help, Gin'l."

"Maybe," the officer conceded grudgingly. "But it's sure a damned nuisance." He turned back to his bedroll and slipped into it while Jack tramped off to care for his horse, rustle something to eat, and bed himself down for the remainder of the night.

Word of his report passed through camp like a blown tumbleweed, electrifying in its import, galvanizing men and officers, and even the stock, except for the mules, bringing new life and drive to the mammoth expedition. By dawn everyone had heard of it. There were fewer complaints than usual as they saddled up and filed out along the trail, now stepping more eagerly, being pulled onward by the promise of combat, the most energizing emotion known to soldiers and to most men.

Throughout the day the command moved forward at a fast walk, trotting a bit now and then, but not too much, since the wagons were hard put to maintain such a pace, unless the ground was favorable. Ravalier impatiently put up with their lumbering movement as long as he could, then halted the entire command.

"Captain Graham!" he called to the officer commanding B Company of the Infantry. When Graham hurried up, Ravalier ordered: "Cut out those wagons, and let them follow along at their own speed. You an' B Company, along with M of the Infantry, escort them forward. The command will push on with the packs, as long as they can keep up, an' when they can't, we'll cut them off, too."

Graham's face fell. He realized he was probably being eliminated from a fight to come. But he was a soldier.

"Yes, sir," he said, reining around and cantering back to his foot soldiers. The company fell back, surrounded the wagons until the command had passed, and then formed up as a guard to bring them along the trail left by the men hurrying toward combat. Combat the Infantrymen would hear about for years to come, but in which they could not share. Military luck.

Freed of the slow-moving wagons, Ravalier hurried the column on, more often at a trot now, his scouts well out in front, examining and charting the way. Late that night, long after dark, they bivouacked on the south bank of the Canadian, with the snow still whipping in, small flakes that meant a probable long fall. The Canadian was mostly dry, but the officer demanded that the column cross it. He was taking no chances on a sudden night flood that might cut them off from their target. No fires could be lighted, despite the abundant firewood, and the men huddled, cold and snow-blown, under their thin blankets, munching hard bread and sipping cold water. Few complained.

Before dawn they were in the saddle again, striking southeast, moving more deliberately now, with greater caution, lest their presence be detected by some stray Cheyennes. But they were fortunate. "Ravalier's luck," the men called it.

Dipsy Jack had gone on ahead, moving more cautiously than ever, but working on, nonetheless. Several other scouts followed some distance behind, maintaining contact both with Jack and with the column. The snow had stopped. Two or three inches lay on the open hills, and a little more in the defiles and under the scattered trees. Moving easterly, and a little southerly, the command had entered country slightly better timbered than the high plains, but still with trees mostly found along the creek beds and river bottoms only.

Shortly before dark Jack rejoined them, making his way directly to Ravalier.

"The camp is over thataway, maybe three, four mile," he said, white breath floating off into the dusk. "I ain't found Gridey yet, but thought you'd like to stop here until she's dark, an' then move on up. That way we kin get within good distance o' th' camp an' hit her when yore ready."

* * *

That same evening, far to the northwest, a buckboard left a westbound freight wagon train, bound south, but not very far south. In it were a young man, the son of the train captain, and red-headed Kim Raggensworth, bundled in warm, cushiony buffalo robes. Warned by his father not to leave the train very far, Stephen Courtney had reassured him.

"I just want to show Fort Zarah to Kim," he had grinned. "She says she's never seen a 'real, stone fort,' is what she says. She'd ought to see one before she gets home to Santa Fe."

The elder Courtney chuckled.

"Especially now that there ain't no garrison there, an' lots of empty buildin's," he approved. "Go along and have a good time, but keep your eyes peeled. Them Cheyennes could be anywhere, even here!"

"Don't worry, pop," replied the son. "Ol' Gimlet Eye— that's me!"

Dust Devil and his war party, too, were approaching Zarah, on the northern bend of the Arkansas. But they were coming up from the southwest.

XVI

Ravalier's attack plan was militarily orthodox. Captain
Murphy, with E Company, would swing around across the
Washita to create a diversion in the rear and bring the
Cheyennes up into their camp from that direction. The main
blow would come from the remaining companies under
Ravalier's command, flooding over the ridge and making
straight into the upper village. Jack had confirmed that there
were more lodges and encampments downstream, he didn't
know how far, or how many, or what their precise location
was. But they extended beyond sight, as far as he had
scouted. Probably all of the Southern Cheyennes were
camped there. Perhaps some Comanches, too, if there were
a temporary alliance between the two peoples, Ravalier
estimated. No matter. If the attack succeeded it would throw
the upper camp into confusion. This, being contagious in an
Indian village, might sweep on to the east.

At any rate, the thing to do was to sweep the upper
village first, and then worry about those lower down.

Murphy and his thirty-two man company slipped away at
2 a.m. on their great circle to the west. They were to reach
a striking position by 4. The attack was to begin with a
trumpet call at 4:30 or 5, depending upon the light. With
a cloudy morning like this one, you could never be sure

when it was going to raise enough to shoot accurately. But
you didn't want too much light, for an enemy was more
confused, and more frightened, by a thundering assault
force pouring in half-seen in the obscurity of faint light,
than he would be by a brightly outlined enemy hitting them
later on. Not to mention the fact that the earlier the attack,
the more Indians would still be drugged by sleep.

"Wish to Christ I had a smoke," muttered Allen
Harrison, behind Vaiking, as he held his impatient horse in
the K Company line. Harrison had wanted to come along,
and Captain Ravalier had let him, although the clerk
normally would have remained at the post.

"Here, have a chaw," drawled Tennessee. "Give you
somethin' to do an' take yore mind off smokin'."

Harrison gratefully accepted the plug. He bit off a fair-
sized chew.

"Only thing is," cautioned Tennessee, "don't swaller it
when you gits excited. You do an' th' excitement from then
on'll be in yore belly, not amongst them Injuns."

"I'll remember," Harrison promised.

Tennessee stamped his feet on the packed snow.

"Sure as hell is cold," he muttered.

The morning stole imperceptibly over the land, but there
was no sound, not even of night birds, or of dogs in the
village beyond the ridge, nor even of coyote or lobo wolf.
The great encampment had frightened away the game, and
the predators had followed it beyond hearing. Even the
horses drowsed, unaware of the demands shortly to be made
upon them. Growling and muttered conversations among
the men had ceased.

At long last, in the growing light, a whispered word came
down the line: "Saddles!" and the men mounted stiffly and
eased their carbines out of the saddle boots. Those fortunate
ones who carried pistols loosened them in the cold leather
holsters. The long line of ranks moved forward, up through
the light dusting of snow and the frosted grass poking
through, brushing the silvered sage, to top out on the ridge,

when, for the first time, Vaiking and the others could see the village with its drift of smoke lying low among the lodges, mixing with similar fogs downstream for a long way. The camp was still as death. No one, nothing moved. It was asleep, even to its dogs and a pony tied here and there among the dwellings.

An old woman wriggled from a lodge in about the middle of the camp, and squatted before the ashes of last night's campfire. She stooped to blow upon the live embers, when her eye apparently caught the movement on the ridge. She straightened, peered more intently, then howled, a long, thin wail that carried from lodge to lodge, stirring their inhabitants to life. She turned to dive into her own tepee when a bullet caught her squarely in the back and flattened her, sprawled her on the packed earth before it. At the same instant the clear notes of Henry's trumpet sounded the charge, and a rattling of carbine fire broke out from among the oncoming horses, the bullets ripping and tearing through the skin lodges like hornets. Indians, a few of them warriors, the others old and young, male and female, children and elders, burst with frightened howls from every lodge, milling, seeking cover, screaming, yelping occasionally with the pain from a sudden wound. Most of the Indians made for the timbered creek bottom, but shots from the other direction indicated that Murphy had reached his position, and was doing his assigned work from there.

The Cavalry thundered down the slope with a clatter of hoofs and the light, staccato yipping of the suddenly warmed troopers, firing their pieces as they came, shooting at anything that moved, irresistible in their charge. They swept through outlying herds of ponies, shooting down a stray boy sent to bring them in, and sending the loose animals, manes tossing and tails flying, plunging away up the river, out of the fight.

A company on the right, upstream from the camp itself, swept through the river, sending showers of ice slivers fountaining upward, and turned down the other bank. Far ahead they could see Murphy's charging troopers rounding a forested bend below the village, aiming, no doubt, to complete the trap.

But the main force, under Ravalier, dashed up to the timber, and swept along the front of the encampment, firing into the lodges, shooting at anything that resembled an Indian, loosing a torrent of lead into the enemy, at the hostile positions, even at no target in particular.

Vaiking found himself swept up in the heat and excitement of the battle, as he always was by action, as he had been throughout his adult life.

He fired with the rest of them, at targets presenting themselves, at the lodges. One warrior from behind a tree bent his bow and loosed an arrow that caught Tennessee full in the chest, dropping him with a heavy grunt from his running horse. He bounced once or twice on the iron soil, rolled over, breaking off the shaft, and lay still, his mouth and eyes open but not breathing. Dead.

The bay horse carried Vaiking plunging across a sandy defile until the Sergeant could see behind the tree where the Indian again had bent his bow, the metal-tipped arrow aimed at the soldier. But Vaiking fired first, flattening the hostile whose dying hands loosened the bowstring and sent the arrow into the sand, where it remained, its feathered tip a bright dot on a bleak landscape.

Harrison caught a bullet in his left arm, not his writing arm, fortunately. But it shattered the bone. He gasped at Vaiking: "I done it! My God, I done it!"

"Done what?" shouted the Sergeant, his teeth bared in the heat of battle. He noticed Harrison's heavy wound.

"Swallered the chew!" gasped Harrison, falling back, his face white, whether from the tobacco in his belly or the wound in his arm Vaiking could not tell. He swept on.

Up and down the stream the shooting, shouting and warfare went on.

Ravalier ordered two companies to round up the loose horses and hold them upstream, to test the Indian strength in that direction, for the cascade of fire had been communicated eastward and roused whatever Indians there were in that direction.

"What about Murphy, sir?" demanded Nero, swinging his lathered horse in beside Ravalier's.

"What about him?" asked Ravalier, surprised, jerking his head around to stare at his First Sergeant. "What's with Murphy? Where is he?"

"I don't know, sir," replied Nero, tensely. "I ain't seen him since th' attack began. I seen his command, or some of it, sweepin' down that way an' behind that point o' trees. They was shootin' over there pretty hot fer a few minutes, but they ain't no shootin' there now. Want me to go see?"

"Go see," ordered Ravalier. "But don't go too far—not out of sight. Keep us in sight, Nero. Don't go too far!" the officer again cautioned. Nero took five men and cantered off, through the shattered village to the other side of the river, and turned downstream.

Ravalier sent most of his remaining force down the left bank of the river, probing toward the villages below, to see how far they could get and what resistance they stirred up. There were horse herds in that direction, too, and he dispatched a few men to see if they could drive the animals off. A dismounted Indian, he knew, was only half a warrior. A few of the men were completing a last sweep through the battered village they had attacked first.

"Captain!" wailed a voice from the interior of that encampment.

"Captain!" it repeated. "Captain, come look here!" It was Gunderson, whose shrill voice, raised above the continuing racket, floated over the lodges and reached the officer where he had paused briefly to assess the field. Ordering Vaiking to fall in beside him, Ravalier spurred toward the wail, past a fallen, crumpled tepee to the center of the village, or where the center had been. He rode up to a knot of men.

"What's the difficulty?" he rasped harshly. "Why did you call me?"

"Captain, look!" gasped Gunderson, pointing to a blob that had once been a man, fastened to a tall stump in the center of the opening.

Its head dropped forward, the sockets where the eyes had been now emptied. Its bones, the long ones, had been broken, one by one, and what Army reports euphemistically referred to as the man's "privates" had been ripped off, stuffed into his mouth. Little was left that resembled a human being, but that little was identifiable. It had been Gridey.

"Looks like they got to 'im," commented Dipsy Jack to no one in particular. He spat a thick, brown stream.

"I tol' th' damn' fool to be keerful," he recalled.

The horror-stricken soldiers cut the leather thongs that had held Gridey upright, and the body sagged to the ground. Vaiking felt sick. But unlike the other men, his anger did not seem aimed at the Indians, even at those still popping shots and flinging arrows at them from time to time. His anger was directed at the war. At the whole bloody business. Somehow, even in the heat of the action, and in the face of the maddening cruelty revealed by the fate of Gridey, he felt detached. It was not the Indians who had done this, he felt, It was conflict. He didn't feel sympathetic toward the Cheyennes. He didn't feel anything. Just a sudden wash of weariness deluging him, a staleness, a feeling that he had seen this all before, a numbing realization that it would go on and on and on forever.

But his fatalistic awareness was not shared by the others. Vaiking sensed an inevitable wave of fury sweep over the men, infecting them, even the Captain. Most of all the officer, in fact. It was as though he knew nothing of the chain of events which had resulted in this gruesome tragedy, as though this were an isolated instance, rising out of the bloodthirsty nature of the Indians, out of the depths of their twisted beings, and not at all in retaliation for cruelties inflicted upon them by the whites.

Ravalier's brown eye all but closed, with the tic hovering over it. The blue glowed brilliantly as he surveyed the scene once more. He noted the tepees still standing among the trees, with bodies here and there, grotesquely scattered about as if some child had dropped rag dolls in odd places across a playground. Indians still were left. Plenty of Indians. There was work remaining to do.

"Vaiking!" he ordered. The soldier rode to him from the other side of the village center.

"Vaiking," ordered Ravalier tautly, "take K Company, what you can gather of it. Sweep this village from lodge to lodge, from upper end to as far as you can go downstream. Burn the tepees. Burn the people! Shoot them. Shoot everything that moves, man or woman, child or white hair. Kill them all! Kill everyone in the village! Kill an' burn until there ain't a hump left anywhere. I want to ride my horse over this place from end to end and not have him even stumble! Burn and kill, Vaiking!"

Vaiking hesitated, stroked his mustache.

At that moment Nero and his detachment swept across the stream and clattered into the clearing.

"Captain," he blurted, "I don' know where th' hell Captain Murphy is. We went to th' point o' trees, and we didn't see him, nor even hear any shootin' down that way. All we seen was Indians! It seemed like every Indian on the plains is makin' up to come this way! But I don't know what happened to the Captain, sir!"

Ravalier surveyed the scene downstream. He couldn't see far because of the screen of trees.

"Murphy's got plenty of men," he decided. "Let him fight his way back."

But Murphy would not get back, nor would his men.

"Nero, take this message to Stanton," said Ravalier. He scribbled something on a sheet of note paper, and handed it to the First Sergeant.

"Wait a minute," he said then. He stared again at Vaiking, still undecided, sitting his bay horse in the clearing, staring at Gridey, but not seeing him. At least, not clearly.

"For God's sake, what's that?" cried Nero, observing the body for the first time.

"That's Gridey, the scout," said Ravalier, not taking his eyes off of Vaiking. "That was Gridey, rather. It's what's left of him."

Nero went over to inspect the corpse at close range. None of the other men had done that.

Ravalier spoke, a low tone that had the weight of authority behind it, the authority of an officer, of a commander of the whole Army, of all military history.

"Vaiking!" he ordered, anger in his voice, the fury of frustration. Maybe there was a touch of guilt in it, too. "Vaiking, take K Company and get started, like I told you!"

Vaiking looked at his commanding officer. This, he knew, was the end. This was the moment of decision. This was when he decided, in the only way he could decide. He could do nothing else.

"No, Captain," he said. "I cannot do it. I guess I ain't no soldier, sir. What you're asking me to do, I can't do. I cannot do it."

"You," said the officer, after a pause, "are under arrest, for disobeyin' a lawful order in the face of the enemy. You know what that means, Vaiking?"

"I know, sir," said the soldier.

"Nero!" bellowed Ravalier. "Take K Company an' sweep this village from right to left, from top to bottom, as far downstream as you can go. Don't leave anyone alive, leave no tepee standing, burn everything and shoot anything that moves, of any age or any sex. *Kill and burn*, Sergeant!"

"Yes, sir," grinned Nero. It was the same grin he had worn when he responded to that order on the Cimarron, Vaiking noted, irrelevantly.

XVII

Nero bore fire and torch to the hapless Indian survivors huddling in their shattered community, but Vaiking turned away, riding into the defile on the north side of the village, dismounted there and sat glumly on a rock while he pondered issues too great for him. At the heart of his reflections, however, was his own role, and what it had become. He clearly recalled the Colonel's words, that "the Army is a tool only," and that the "end of everything is man."

That being true, he thought, why all this? The fight to control the village was clearly justifiable, but once captured, why descend to murder and pillage upon the helpless remnants? That could only be one more link in the bloody circle of injury and retaliation and revenge and more retaliation, going on forever. It was basically that which he felt he could no longer be a part of, and to avoid which he had now finally sacrificed his role in the Army, perhaps his life.

He could never go back, and neither, he knew, would Ravalier who held now the power of life and death over him, although there were certain necessary processes he must go through before he could act.

Vaiking's thoughts were interrupted by whoops and the

clatter of hoofs from downstream, and he mounted barely in time to avoid being run down by nearly one thousand Indian ponies, being driven west at a dead run by Captain Chapman and the shouting troops sent down earlier to probe the camps easterly along the river bottoms.

Chapman cantered over to Ravalier while his men circled the immense herd and held it on the flats just north of the upper end of the village.

"There's plenty of Indians down there, Ravalier!" reported Chapman, his horse dancing and stepping nervously back and forth, hot and impatient from the long drive. "They're making medicine, or whatever they do, and we can expect them up here pretty damn soon!"

Dipsy Jack, who had scouted east after the main body of troops, also galloped up.

"We is gonna be drowned in Injuns right quick, Gin'l!" he announced.

A thin trumpet call from the herd holders brought them to attention.

"Here they come!" shouted Chapman, spurring his horse into the defile and across its sandy, graveled bottom, its iron shoes ringing on loose stones. Chapman scrambled his mount up the cutbank on the other side and he galloped off to rejoin his command. After him sped Vaiking, still armed although under arrest. In this situation every man counted. Behind them Ravalier was mustering K Company to bring it into the action. Chapman rapidly dismounted his men and sent them to form skirmish lines to left and right, seeking what cover they could find. Other commanders north of him did the same.

From the east, coming in an endless file from the cottonwoods along the Washita, came the painted, feathered Indians of camps lower down the river, most on horseback but with dismounted stragglers hurrying to keep pace. They came singing their weird songs, their lance-tips glowing in the early light, a few already popping their guns in aimless shooting, but most of them businesslike, determined.

"God! Look at 'em come! They must be a million of 'em!" breathed a soldier, hugging the frozen ground to Vaiking's left.

"Quite a few, all right," he agreed. "Discipline will count here. If we hold our ground and fire low, I doubt if they run over us."

"A million of 'em!" marveled the soldier.

"They won't seem so many when they come in on us," predicted Vaiking. "Some of 'em won't join the charge at all, but they'll mill, looking for some advantage with no cost, like stealin' back the horses. All we got to do is stop the first charge, if we can."

The warriors drew up six hundred yards downstream, spreading out north and south, forming a line nearly half a mile wide, a beautiful, barbaric sight. One rider, wearing only a couple of long white eagle feathers in his black hair and mounted on a white pony with a brown spot covering its right eye, rode on to the front, coming to within three hundred yards of the waiting troopers. He bore a lance and raised it high over his head, turned his pony and rode north, along the front of the soldiers, his war song ringing around them, his pony loping slowly, unhurried. At the north end of the soldiers' line he turned and loped back toward the south.

"What th' hell's he doin'?" wondered the soldier alongside Vaiking.

"That's what they call 'emptyin' the soldiers' guns,'" replied the Sergeant. "He's a brave man, an' he thinks his medicine is strong this mornin'. He don't think he'll get hit—an' he don't care much if he does."

He marveled at the grace of the rider, as soldiers up and down the line, not waiting for orders, began to shoot at him. The bullets sent up puffs of sand and gravel to front and rear of the pony, but none seemed to find its target. The Indian spun his horse at the south end of the line, where his route reached the timber, and rode back across the front. More guns were opened on him now, but he seemed to bear a charmed life.

One bullet struck the horse at last, in the left hindquarter, spinning it partly around. The Indian rode the maneuver with ease, corrected the course of the animal and loped on. At the north end of his route, he pulled away and galloped easily back to the Indian line, joining three or four leaders clustered a few yards ahead of it, about at its center. The soldier fire ceased.

"His medicine is strong today," grunted Vaiking.

The barbaric line began to move forward now, coming on at a walk, steadily, purposefully, lance feathers fluttering. It seemed an eternity before they covered half the distance to the soldiers. The troopers held their fire, shrinking closer to the earth, if possible, weapons ready, watching the gorgeous, terrifying spectacle.

"They ain't only Cheyennes there; they's Comanches, too, an' a few Kiowas," muttered Dipsy Jack to Ravalier, on the right of the soldier line. "They must be seven, eight hundred of 'em. I didn't think they could git that many Injuns together on th' south plains fer ration issuance, let alone a fight."

The soldiers' horses had been led back into the timber behind them, where the horse-holders watched the spectacle from what amounted to ringside seats. But if the Indians broke through, they would have their hands full enough.

At three hundred yards, half the distance to the soldiers, the Indian line drew up momentarily. The warrior on the white pony again raised his lance, threw back his head and roared out his war cry.

The call was taken up and echoed in rippling screams up and down the long enemy line, quavering, high-pitched, penetrating, chilling. The Indian dug his heels into his pony which leaped ahead. The entire hostile band surged forward, first at a lope and now at a mad run, pounding down upon the prone soldiers in a slashing assault that seemed utterly irresistible. The troopers' fire opened with a roar and then settled into staccato monotones as they fired and reloaded their single-shot pieces as fast as each man could do so.

Indians toppled from their ponies, but not so many as later reports would claim. The soldiers, too, were excited, and some fired high. Only the cool men, the experienced for the most part, made their shots count in the beginning. The warriors pressed home their grand attack, and created the start of turmoil. No one knew who was firing at whom, or even for sure that he held a man in his sights.

The warriors drove at a blistering gallop straight into the mouths of the soldiers' guns. A few leaped their horses over the white line, making for the held pony herds to the rear. Most of the fighters, though, milled, seeking combat with the troopers, causing them casualties as well as taking some, but intent only on the battle, the fight, the individual combat, the counting of coups to boast about later on around the fires in the lodges. The left of the soldier line was driven in and fell back toward the center. But the middle and the right, where the ground was rougher, held firm. The outcome was uncertain. The balance likely would be held by the force most determined.

It evolved into a multitude of individual combats, man against man, man against horse, pistol against bow, rifle against lance. Every man's courage was decisive in his particular battle.

At this moment Vaiking, with one bullet left in his pistol, rose up to face the warrior on the white pony, an immense rider, painted, contemptuous of danger, bearing in on him at a thundering gallop. The Indian's lance was raised and he thrust it directly at Vaiking, who barely dodged, clutched it, and jerked the Indian from his mount. He landed on his back with a thud heard above the sound of combat, and bounced up, wresting his lance from the Sergeant's grasp, lifting it once more to ram its saber point into the great white soldier. But he was not swift enough. The remaining bullet from the Sergeant's pistol caught him full in the face, flung his body backwards to lie in a crumpled heap amid the milling maelstrom of battle.

A shriek, almost a wail, rose from nearby Indians who

had seen the encounter, a peal taken up by others across the tumultuous battlefield, the lament that their leader and bravest warrior was gone, slain, that his medicine had given out, that this day from now on was truly evil for war. They bolted, leaving the shattered, fractured lines of soldiers to reform, fleeing on their scampering ponies toward the villages below, to fight no more this day. As they left their wail drifted after them, a sad, wild, piercing sound, but to the exhausted soldiers a cry of triumph.

"Thet was right close," said Dipsy Jack calmly to Ravalier. "I thought they had us good."

"I did, too," agreed the officer.

"They would of made tepee decorations out of most of us, if Vaiking hadn't of nailed ol' Buffalo Hump like he done."

"That his name? I wondered who he was."

"Supposed to be th' greatest fightin' man th' Comanches had," said Jack quietly. "Without him, they didn't have no stomach to keep on fightin'." He chewed reflectively. "He's th' reason, I reckon, why th' Comanches joined in this fight. He wanted to, an' all them that follered him come along because he did. Wal, they won't foller him no more, that's certain."

The two walked over to the group clustered around the fallen body of Buffalo Hump.

"Was you a Injun, Vaiking, you'd have a passel of coups fer toppin' off that one," approved Jack. The soldier grinned.

"But being as you're not an Indian, Vaiking," said Ravalier grimly, "you're still under arrest for disobeying an order in the face of the enemy. Report to Nero. Give him your weapons, and if he wants to take your stripes, give them to him, too."

"Yes, sir," said Vaiking evenly, turning away.

He collected his bay, mounted and hunted up Nero. The First Sergeant watched him as he let the horse pick its way carefully across the draw, mount the bank and approach. Vaiking removed his belt, with the shot pouches, and holstered pistol, and handed them without a word to the other.

"What the hell's this, hero?" demanded the noncom. His astonishment was genuine enough.

Vaiking shrugged.

"I'm on the Captain's list again, Nero," he admitted. "He put me under arrest and told me to report to you. It's your turn, now."

Nero, hating Vaiking, still was a soldier, a good one, and he sympathized with the other but he would never show it.

"I'll be damned," he said, taking the belt. "A man never knows, in this Army. He might git a medal, an' he might git busted. But I never before seen a man aimin' at both fer one day's work."

He called Gunderson and Woody over.

"This here ain't your company Sergeant no more," he said. "He's your prisoner. Guard him like you would your life, or the Captain'll skin you alive. Take him over by that creek bank yonder an' keep him there fer a week, if you have to, until the Captain figures out what he's gonna do with him. Only don't let him git out of your sight, an' don't let him go, because if you do, you'll git on the list, too. An' there ain't no pleasure in that, leave me tell you!"

Vaiking sat on a knoll, in the warming sunlight, feeling tired and not much of anything else after the hard morning's work. Woody was glum. Gunderson, too, was silent.

"Whatever you done, Sarge, to git the Captain down on you so?" demanded Woody. He, like most of the company, had come to like Vaiking, and he looked up to him as he had never admired anyone before in his spotted, urban slum life.

"He told me to do something, an' I couldn't do it, so he put me under wraps like I am."

"Aw, wait'll he cools off, Vaiking. You're too damn good a soldier to be done away with, permanent."

"A good soldier does what he's told," answered Vaiking

dully. "I got so I can't do that all the time any more. So I ain't a good soldier no more. The Captain can't understand me, either. Neither of us can. All I know is, I'm gettin' to be a hell of a soldier, and the Captain can't make a good one out of me, so here I set."

He stared morosely across the draw at the pony herd, spread out now and grazing up the slopes of the ridge. Ravalier was talking with other officers on the scene of the late battle. Details were collecting the bodies of the soldier dead, but those of the slain Indians, scattered about the field, were left to lay. It looked like Gettysburg all over again, Vaiking thought, only he guessed it wasn't so bad as Gettysburg, at that. Some improvement!

Ravalier had turned now from the other officers and was coming toward the burned, smoking site of the former village, where even more Indian dead were scattered, most of them—almost all, in fact—women and children. Nero's detachment had spared no one, as the Captain had ordered.

Far out on the field the officers mustered their companies. They detailed units under noncommissioned officers. These elements scattered to right and left, making for the pony herd, gradually circling it, driving the multicolored animals toward the center, making the herd compact and tight.

Ravalier rode past Vaiking without a word. He hunted up Nero.

"Muster K Company and have them make bivouac out there on the flat, away from the timber," he directed. "We ain't going no place further today. I don't think the Indians will attack again today, or tonight, and neither does Jack. We're going to shoot the pony herd, so that will remove that incentive for a night raid. But picket our horses and mules good, out away from the trees."

"Yes, sir," said Nero.

"Establish a double guard too. You don't have to tell them to keep their eyes peeled; I guess they know that. The other companies will bivouac out there, too. We'll head back tomorrow, unless the Indians want more fight. Jack doesn't think they will, though, not with Hump gone."

"Yes, sir."

Ravalier rode back out of the ruined village, across the draw, up on the flat. Again he passed Vaiking without speaking to him or looking at him. It was as though his ex-Company Sergeant did not exist. More likely, it was because he still hadn't made up his mind what to do with him. About him.

He stared curiously at Buffalo Hump as he rode past him, the Indian staring with sightless eyes at the clear sky, one arm thrown across his chest, the other flung out toward the pony herd, still being collected.

About 2 p.m. the killing started.

Three companies, formed with troopers single file, circled the great herd, each man with a loaded pistol, and each company headed by a First Sergeant. An officer nodded and the shooting began. It sounded from a distance like corn in a skillet, popping away against the lid. The long line of troopers circled round and round the herd, each man shooting into it; reloading, and firing again and again and again. Mostly they aimed for head shots, but some for the body. The horses fell, by tens, scores, hundreds. The plains were littered with dead ponies, the narrowing circle of troopers had difficulty finding foot room among the carcasses. Still the shooting continued. The herd itself, wild at first, seemed to little realize what was happening to it, and the ponies, heads up and ears pointed, manes drifting with the light breeze, waited each its turn.

"God, it's awful!" gritted Woody.

Gunderson watched silently. He hadn't spoken since assigned to this job. He never said much, though.

"Awful!" Woody said again, to himself.

"It ain't pretty," agreed Vaiking. "But as long as we keep them horses alive, they'd be sure bait for the warriors, and we'd have one raid after another, all night long an' until we get back to Chips. This way maybe they'll leave us alone."

"Maybe," conceded Woody.

The shooting continued until only a scattered handful of horses remained standing. Soldiers behind the circling line were shooting wounded animals, more to put them out of misery than to complete the slaughter.

A final group of half a dozen horses broke through the lines, bounded off across the prairie, a trooper or two in hard-pounding pursuit of each, running them down like buffalo. Two horses got away, apparently unwounded, galloping freely westward, away from camp. Their pursuers returned at last, admitting defeat.

"Let them go," said Ravalier. "Two horses won't stir up a raid. We weren't 'punishing' them, anyway. Just eliminating them."

He turned to Captain Chapman, who was noting figures in his book.

"How many do you make, Chapman?" he asked.

"One thousand, four hundred sixty-two shot, and two got away. Total according to my count is one thousand, four hundred sixty-four."

"Good day's work," said Ravalier. "We better get supper an' complete our camps. We'd ought to pull out at about dawn."

"Right," replied Captain Chapman.

As the afternoon waned, Vaiking had become more thoughtful. His attention had been focused for a time on the horse slaughter going on across the flats, but now that was over. Only the fallen bodies of the hundreds of animals dotted the plains where earlier they had grazed and freely roamed. Vaiking turned once more to considering his own plight. He thought, for the first time in recent hours, of Josiah Pickerfield and what he had said. Vaiking speculated on his own future, now bleak enough. He thought of the Army, his home for so many years, and of his career as a soldier. Finally, he made his decision.

It was dark now, the early prewinter dusk had closed in. The plains lay still and white under the night sky, except where the warm sun of the day had burned off patches of snow, leaving dark stains of bare earth, brush and rock. From far down the river came the ghost of chanting from the Indian camps, where women, no doubt, were keening for their lost husbands, sons and brothers. There would be no attack this night, though the soldiers took no risks.

"Gunderson," said Vaiking, at last, "I got to go to the can. Take me up this bottom aways."

Gunderson obligingly got stiffly to his feet and walked behind Vaiking, as he dropped into the draw and moved up it beyond the bivouac area. He unbuckled his belt, squatted, and when he rose, brought up a rounded rock in his right hand. He buckled the belt again, and stepped past Gunderson. As he did so, he whirled and crashed the rock into the soldier's temple, felling him like a pole-axed ox.

"Sorry," he muttered as he stooped over, swiftly gathering up Gunderson's carbine and pistol belt, buckling the latter around him, and slipping rapidly through the night toward the picket line. He came up behind a guard, struck him neatly under the ear with his pistol, then picked up his own saddle and blanket, carefully saddled his bay, slipped on a bridle, and led the horse from the picket line, out beyond the camp, to the center of a dark patch. There he mounted and turned his horse toward the north.

He walked the animal from camp to a safe distance, then spurred him into a long, easy lope, and rode for the north star. He left a plain trail, but he did not worry about it. No horse in the regiment could catch the bay, given a night's start. For the first time in many a month, Vaiking felt wholly free.

XVIII

Dust Devil, Big Ass and their sixty-four fighting men had ridden thirty-eight hours without pause since the affair on the Arkansas. It was not much of a victory. But added to depredations farther east, it provided a satisfactory finale to the last expedition of the season, and besides, it had come to the climax Dust Devil wished above all.

The snows would soon come and the grass be too little, too hard to reach, to keep a war pony in condition, and that was why this would be the final raid.

During the long months to come the horses would have to be fed cottonwood twigs and bark, or starve until spring, when their strength, if they survived, would return with the warming sun, melting snows, and growing grass. It had always been thus. This recent journey had sapped the strength from them, down to the final reserves necessary to reach the people camped on the Washita. There the women could care for them during the cold months, and the men could rest, conduct their ceremonials, boast of their great deeds, and plan new feats to come with the end of the hard times of winter.

Now they had this redheaded woman with them. They had seized her when they slew her companion amid the stone-walled ruins of that old soldier post near the creek called Walnut by the whites, named for the trees along its banks. It emptied into the Arkansas. The clash in which the white man was killed and his woman captured had been swift and successful, in that there was no loss among the Indians. The warriors were happy about it.

Most gleeful was Dust Devil, who personally had tomahawked the man and, wrapping her long red hair around his muscular fingers, had swung the woman out of the buckboard and dragged her wildly across the prairie and through the shallow Arkansas a safe distance south. There they mounted the scarcely conscious woman on a stolen pony, and had ridden rapidly southwest, making no attempt to cover their trail, since they moved so swiftly and the snows would soon blot out all trace of it. They had made one camp, along the Medicine Lodge River, where Dust Devil had had his fill of the white woman and turned her over to Big Bear and Spotted Wolf for their amusement. They had passed her along to others. But the halt had been too brief for many to use her. They mounted up, taking the woman with them still, because Dust Devil insisted upon it. Now they were sweeping on toward the Cimarron.

Dust Devil seemed rarely to take his eyes from the captive. When she roused herself from the dull-bronze-tasting emptiness to a dim awareness of her surroundings and circumstances, Kim was vaguely conscious of this attention. Being a woman, she hazily identified it with desire, and with her body. But sometimes there seemed in the gleam of his black eyes some other emotion, something like revenge. She did not speculate about it. She did not wonder about anything. For the first time, and perhaps the last time in her life, she did not think of herself as a person, as a being all-important, to herself at any rate, but rather as a trapped and hopelessly doomed unit of the race, all vanity bludgeoned aside, face to face with bare realities which seemed to have no remote resemblance to what had passed for "realities" in the long lifetime ago when she had been simply a desirable woman, adventuring among desiring men.

So the cavalcade clattered southward. Most of the warriors left her alone. She was not mistreated except sexually, although handled very roughly. When the warriors paused to kindle their small fires and roast some meat, she was given a chunk of it. Her horse was as strong and as fleet as the others. Some Indian saw to it she had a saddle, when most of them rode with only a thin blanket between the pony's back and their own hardened rumps. One warrior even hammered down a protruding rivet that had cut into her leg from the stirrup strap and was causing her excruciating pain. Not until long afterward did the realization dawn on her that he had muttered, "That's better," when he finished, and she had been so unconscious of it at the time that she could not locate him later, even had she possessed the initiative and determination to do it. Most of the warriors ignored her, although they jested among themselves and were ever alert and watchful of their surroundings.

North of the Cimarron they encountered the first strips of white remaining from the snow to the south, although much of it had melted and the river itself was up slightly. But they did not get to cross it.

As the main group swung down toward the stream, two or three warriors who had been in the advance stopped and chattered excitedly, pointing to the earth. Even Kim, in her dazed and not wholly responsible state, could see that they were discussing a trail of a single horse, coming up out of the river bottom, striking north. What had excited their interest, although she could not know this, nor would she have cared if she had, was that the tracks were very fresh, with water still collected in them, that they were of a shod horse, and therefore neither a wild animal nor one ridden by an Indian, and, above all, that the horse had gone lame, proven by one consistently deeper track than those of its other hoofs.

This meant to them that a lone white man was nearby, hindered by a crippled horse. They might easily add one more scalp to the array they now possessed. With yips of excitement the warriors, or most of them, raced out on the trail, leading toward the hill country a mile or so north of the river. The chief shouted something at them as they left, and they heard him, and responded, and then went on.

Joel Vaiking heard his pursuers before he saw them. He clapped spurs to the bay, knowing while he did so that it was futile. But it was the only thing he could do. Since picking up a rock south of the river, the deep-bottomed animal had become very lame. It responded bravely to the spur, but it was a hopeless effort, and Vaiking knew it. Yet he turned the horse's head toward a stony hill, standing southerly from the main ridge. There he might make a stand. He had still a carbine and pistol, and pouches half full of cartridges. There was a glimmer of a chance if he could stand them off for a day or two. They might weary of the unrewarding fight. Perhaps, too, some military outfit might swing north from the Washita, and drive them off.

That was at best a desperate possibility. Vaiking was not given to illusions. But at a time like this, it was a man's nature to hope.

He had intended pushing north for the emigrant routes. There he could easily sell the horse and, if necessary, his arms, and take a stage either for the settlements back east or the mining camps of Colorado or even California, if his money held out. There always was work there. A man's identity was only what he cared to reveal. The camps were where most Army deserters went. Vaiking, much as he detested the label, knew that now he was a deserter and, in the army's view, nothing more.

He might make a new, and perhaps reasonably satisfactory, life for himself in the camps, whether he ever amassed much of the earth's riches or not. But his immediate concern, naturally, was simply to get beyond the reach of the Army, to some place where he could get by, and the future would develop out of itself. With the Indians behind him, and a lame horse under him, however, the future appeared to be directly in hand. There was not much of it.

Vaiking had felt cold and lonely during the long night, but he was warm enough now. Assuredly he had no reason to feel lonely any more.

The first pursuers were in sight now, riding swiftly and lightly on their painted, caparisoned ponies. His bay moved ever more slowly, and the hill seemed very far away. The Indians gained swiftly. By the time he reached the base of the rise they had swung out to either side, and had all but cut him off. Behind them came more, also riding fast, but not pressing too close. They were playing with him, trying to head him off, encircle him. Then they would tease and torment and torture and finally kill him as suited their mood, their playfulness, in their own good time.

But he was part way up the hill now. It wasn't so very high, but high enough. The bay was finished. Vaiking dropped from its back, giving it an affectionate slap on the rump as he clambered on up the incline. The bay had been a good horse, had served him well, and now was through. So, he felt, was he. Both were done—but not quite yet. The horse had stopped almost immediately, raising its sore, off-hind foot to ease its suffering, standing head down, blowing, finished as much by the injury and pain as by the long run.

Vaiking swung behind a boulder and got off two well-aimed shots, one to either side. That to his right dropped an Indian, but only wounded him, although it caused his companions to veer off. The shot to the left killed a pony, and sent its rider sprawling, head foremost. Vaiking turned and scrambled on up the hill.

He gained the summit, blowing hard, and found it flat for a few feet around, and plenty of jagged, loose limestone chunks. While the Indians collected themselves below the hill, he stacked a few stones around, making a rude breastwork. Not much. Not really effective. But it might help. Besides it was something to do besides worry. He was in a spot, and he knew it well.

The soldier had more time than he had supposed. The Indians gathered down below the hill, a few looking up occasionally, but the rest silent except perhaps for low conversations Vaiking could not hear from this distance. One or two worked on foot up the base of the slope a little way, to one side or the other. Vaiking did not waste bullets on them, but went on working up his defenses. What were they waiting for? The two Indians who had started up the hill now were seated comfortably on either side, within a couple of hundred yards. He could have killed either or both of them, but it wouldn't do much good. They weren't threatening him. They seemed to consider themselves mere sentinels. Making sure he didn't leave. Fine chance, leaving! Where would he go? He worked on. The Indians waited.

At last Vaiking used up the last of the stones within reach, and lay behind the parapet, gazing at the scene below, at the knot of Indians, still gesticulating, talking, doing nothing.

Far back toward the river a movement caught his eye. More Indians were coming slowly along the trail. It must be the warrior-leader, Vaiking thought. Why were they awaiting him?

Dust Devil had a firm grip on the halter rope of Kim Raggensworth's horse, leading him on along the trail made by the pursuing Indians toward the north. Far ahead she could see the ridge, and in front of it a rounded hill. At its base was a band of Indians, those warriors who had taken off so excitedly on the trail they had discovered such a short time before. Dimly Kim knew this, in her half-conscious mind, but it was meaningless to her. Passively she rode along, thinking nothing, feeling nothing, largely unaware of the grim reality around her.

Yet she was not entirely unconscious, either. She knew

when they approached the band of warriors ahead. She was aware that they spoke fervently, in their guttural, incomprehensible language to their leader, who held the rope of her horse, and who had abused her first, as was his right. That seemed so long ago, and so damned unimportant now, when everything was unimportant and downhill and gloom, like a sinking bog into which she was moving with men over whom, for the first time in her life, she felt she had no control whatever. She didn't know why she had been brought here, and she didn't even wonder about it. Nothing could be explained any more to make a living pattern for her. Nothing any more, at all.

She felt nothing, no astonishment, not even any pain when, as they reached the base of the hill, Dust Devil suddenly brought her horse beside his, reached over and again wound his fingers in her streaming, thick hair and boosted her over his own pony to the ground, on its left side, where she was suspended, neither on her knees nor on her feet, but midway between, eyes half open, seeing only his lower legs, the belly of his pony, and the rocky slope before her.

From his barricade, Joel Vaiking watched the scene below, puzzled, his mind trying to comprehend what was being enacted below him, attempting to make sense of it all. He was three hundred yards distant from the drama. He could not recognize the woman prisoner from that point, but he knew that she was white. He was aware that the warriors had brought her up for a purpose, and that he was the focal point of that intent.

Dust Devil kicked his pony and guided it forward now, up the slope, at a walk, dragging the white woman with him easily, the great muscles of his bare left arm standing out, his grip on her hair that of iron itself. His face was expressionless. His eyes, if Joel could have seen them, were implacable, cold, relentless.

Upward he came, his pony blowing a bit, picking its way

among the rocks, the white woman stepping a little from time to time, but mostly being dragged as casually as if she had been a buffalo robe, and as effortlessly, too, by the powerful warrior.

They came to within one hundred yards of Vaiking's position, and the woman in dull anguish turned her face upward, and the soldier for the first time felt a twinge of recognition. He couldn't be sure. It resembled to some degree the face of Kim Raggensworth of the Westport-bound train, the gloriously beautiful and wanton Kim Raggensworth with whom he had made love, whose body he had enjoyed, who had aroused his anger when she turned from him to the Captain, and later to others, for that was her nature.

In surprise Vaiking raised his head above the parapet, and that was the movement Dust Devil apparently desired. He pulled his pony up, and with his left arm raised the woman to a standing position, where she swayed, and would have fallen, had his grip on her hair loosened. But it did not.

Dust Devil laid the jaw rope of his pony across its neck, and silently loosed the stone-headed tomahawk from his right side. He stared at Vaiking, said something in Cheyenne to him. Dust Devil whirled the tomahawk once around his head and smashed it with all his strength into the skull of Kim Raggensworth, shattering the bone and spraying her brains on his left leg and the side of his startled pony, loosening his grip and letting her body fall away from him.

Involuntarily Vaiking raised up at the sudden, brutal slaying, aimed his carbine full at Dust Devil's broad chest, and tightened his finger around the trigger. But he did not squeeze it.

There washed across his memory in a split second the words of Josiah Pickerfield, the aged Quaker: "Somebody's got to break the ring. It can be one man. But *somebody* must!"

In an instant Vaiking saw the true meaning of the old man's words—the vicious circle of offense and revenge, and offense and revenge, and still more revenge. It must be broken, or there could be no justice and no peace. And it could not come without a sacrifice on someone's part. He was the man. He was on the target. Dust Devil might never understand. No matter. It had to be done, because he, Vaiking, understood. He could not himself bring peace. But he could fulfill his own understanding. He must do what one man could do.

Slowly Vaiking rose to his feet, facing Dust Devil. He clutched his carbine by the barrel and hurled it seventy feet down the slope of the hill.

"Shoot, goddam it!" he growled.

From the band of milling Indians below came the inevitable hail of arrows and bullets, a blizzard of death, and it was over.

XIX

With his broken leg in its cast propped on a wooden chair before him, Colonel Henry Tangle sat beside the window where the afternoon sunlight was strongest, and read through Captain Karl Ravalier's report of the Washita action. It had been referred to him for any comments he desired to make before sending it to Fort Leavenworth Then it would go to Chicago, and ultimately to Washington where, one day, it would rest in the archives of the nation.

Tangle read carefully, and particularly noted the final paragraph:

"Upon returning to this post," it said, "the command marched north, crossing the Cimarron River a short distance east of the Antelope Hills. We came here on the 6th inst., upon the bodies of a young white woman, reportedly one named Kimberly Raggensworth, the daughter of the acting governor of New Mexico Territory, and a soldier and past noncommissioned officer, Joel Vaiking. They were found on a small hill, approximately three miles north of the river where signs indicated they had made a stand after being cut off by hostile Indians. How the young woman reached that position has not been determined, although it is thought she was captured near the former Fort Zarah, on the Arkansas, on or about the 28th ultimo. Vaiking had deserted the night before from K Company, 12th Cavalry, and presumably was in flight when overtaken. The command returned without further incident to this post where the body of the Raggensworth woman awaits direction from next of kin."

The Colonel glanced up from the report and stared through the hospital window at the parade ground, the dun-colored buildings, all so familiar, and at the bleak Kansas plains beyond. He reflected a long time. Then he lifted up a writing board and laid it on his lap, took some paper and a pen, and began to write a lengthy endorsement to Ravalier's report. He wrote it in the vigorous but unmilitary style for which he was noted.

"I feel constrained to comment further on the last part of Captain Ravalier's report before sending it on to higher authority," he wrote. "The main body of his report is approved, but singular circumstances concerning its ultimate comments require enlightenment from me.

"As I reported by courier yesterday, there came to Fort Arnold Chopps earlier that day, November 11th, three important Indians—Dust Devil, war chief of the hostile band of Cheyennes; Big Ass, a leading warrior of that band; and George Bent, a well-known Cheyenne fighting man whose father, William Bent, founded the famed fort of that name in Colorado Territory many years ago, and whose mother, Owl Woman, was of the Cheyenne tribe. I do not need to go into the mistreatment and cruelties inflicted upon the Bent boy by unprincipled whites which led him to war against our people. He is, however, bilingual, and perfectly at home both with his chosen people, the Cheyennes, and with the whites and, surprisingly enough, is accepted by both equally well.

"I explain all of this as background and authority for what I now report.

"Dust Devil said, through Bent, that the late war which has caused many hundreds of lives to be lost and millions of dollars in damage to property and in expenses connected with military operations, was caused because of the ravishment and murder of his woman some time ago, and his determination for revenge, as well as the generally unsatisfactory condition of the Indians which so unsettled them that a single incident such as this could provoke a major conflict.

"I need not go into further details, except to say that Dust Devil captured the Raggensworth woman, as he would have captured any other, with some dim notion of squaring accounts, and did so, murdering her within sight of the soldier on the hill, Vaiking.

"I would here like to say a word about this soldier. He was known to me.

"I do not know the precise reason for his desertion, if such it was, although I have my suspicions, but I know him for a brave and worthy soldier, of excellent mind and tested loyalty over a great span of years, including the late rebellion where he served with such distinction that he won the Medal of Honor at Gettysburg. I do not think he would 'desert' except under extreme provocation.

"Bent tells me, however, that when Dust Devil killed the woman, within plain sight of Vaiking, the soldier raised up to fire at Dust Devil, and then apparently changed his mind and threw away his carbine and stood defenseless to receive the bullets and arrows of the hostiles. One can only surmise why he did this, but it was not the act of a coward, but of a brave man.

"Furthermore, it is fortunate that he did so. If he had killed Dust Devil, as he easily might have done since the Indian was not in a position to either escape or return the fire, it would have left the Cheyenne faction, now for war, without a leader strong enough to hold them together, and the establishment of peace with that fiery and implacable people might be a matter of many months more and numerous further military operations.

"As it was, however, Dust Devil seems placated by his 'revenge,' and by his assassination of the woman in payment, as he sees it, for the death of his own woman. He has thus listened to Big Ass, captured (through the courageous and intelligent action of said soldier, Vaiking, incidentally), who was sent back with an invitation from Special Indian Commissioner Josiah Pickerfield and myself for Dust Devil to come in and talk. No action was taken on that urging by the Indian, until he had completed the 'revenge' which is so important to the savage mind. That has now been done, and he is ready to talk peace, and I am confident that this bloody war, so fraught with dangerous implications, can speedily be brought to a conclusion.

"It will be seen that this happy result will have been brought about largely, if not entirely, by the action of the soldier, Vaiking, termed a 'deserter' in the report here appended. I do not believe he deserves that appellation as his final characterization by the military of which he was so distinguished a part. There is, I am aware, little that can be done for him at this date, since he left no next of kin according to our records. But I have taken the liberty of ordering Ravalier to send a detail to the scene of his last fight, to disinter the body and bring it to the post here for proper burial. That is the very least that can be done.

"Captain Ravalier's report is otherwise approved. His request for a transfer to the 13th Cavalry, now headquartered at Fort Lincoln, Dakota Territory, is also approved and strongly recommended. If approved by higher authority, travel orders will be issued.

"I am, Sir, yr most obt svt,
"Henry L. Tangle, Col. Comdg., Brevet Maj. Gen."

Josiah Pickerfield at that moment was concluding his own report to the Board of Peace Commissioners, referring to what he termed his mission's "complete, if delayed, success."

"What brought about this happy result," he wrote laboriously, the thin pen point scratching out the words on the ruled, white paper, "was the determination of one man, and one man alone, to break the lamentable chain of revenge and counterrevenge which has plagued Indian-white relations on this continent for hundreds of years. That man, the soldier, Joel Vaiking, and I had held several serious talks about the necessity for this act of self-sacrifice and, while it can never be ascertained now what was in his mind during those final moments when he faced the chief of the hostile band, I am confident that something of the sort must have occurred to him. Otherwise his action is inexplicable. I believe he should be paid this quiet tribute for the justice he will have brought about and the peace which will no doubt follow, with its manifest blessings to both red man and white.''

That night, in her adobe laundry which she had so shut off from all "visitors," Kate Shannon lay on the bed she had so often shared with Joel Vaiking and felt the new life within her. Somehow she *knew* it was his, and just as certainly she was positive it would be a son—a son who would grow into a strapping, blond giant, the image of his father, her man, the only man she had ever, truly, loved.

"May you be as he was," she breathed into the darkness of the quiet room. "May you continue his life, the life he had.

"Oh, Joel, I loved you so!"